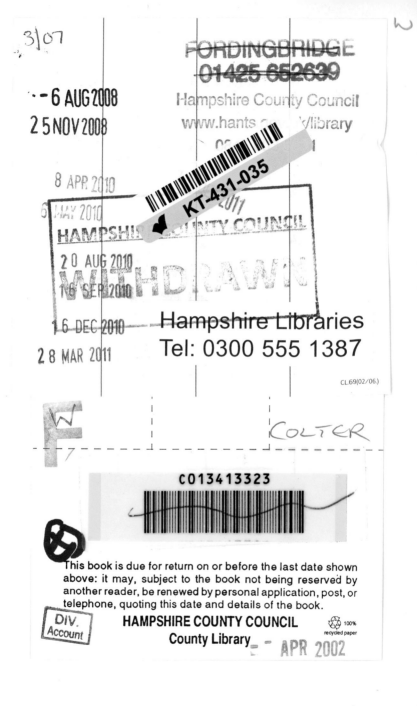

BLOOD ON THE RANGE

Feud raged like wildfire—an old feud, a blood feud—and out of Great Lost Valley rode Gage Hardin to corner one of Louis Peele's gunhawks in the lonely desert. Meanwhile, Peele raided the Circle Crossbar—ruthlessly killing Gage's horses, gunning his best men, stealing his sweetheart, Mary Silver . . .

Gage hit the backtrail with blazing six-shooters, gunfight following gunfight as he blasted through the leadslingers between himself and Peele. Gage meant to shoot his way into a final showdown—*but could he shoot his way out again?*

BLOOD ON THE RANGE

Eli Colter

GUNSMOKE

This hardback edition 2002
by Chivers Press
by arrangement with
Golden West Literary Agency

ISBN 0 7540 8166 4

British Library Cataloguing in Publication Data available.

Printed and bound in Great Britain by
BOOKCRAFT, Midsomer Norton, Somerset

Blood on the Range

CHAPTER I

BEHIND THE HILL

THE open space in which they had reined up was scarcely ten feet in diameter, but it was wide enough for tragedy to stalk. The two men were face to face, motionless, clearly outlined by the moonlight; moonlight so strong that it cast black shadows across the prickly pear and sand.

Silently they sat there a moment, both men shaken by the bitter news one had winded his mount in order to bring —Gage Hardin, young owner of the Circle Crossbar in Great Lost Valley, and his slightly older partner, Doe Gaston. Aside from the spot where their horses stood, there was not a rod of ground but had some cover. Either the dark foliage of spruce on the foothills and leading higher, or the varied green of mesquite or scrub oak or thorn bush that would stop abruptly a little further on, at the mouth of the canyon, where the desert would begin.

But neither of the two mounted men were thinking now of the beauty of the spot, nor of moonlight night nor of the breeze, so grateful after the heat of the day; a breeze that gently waved the brims of their Stetsons, softly ruffled the horses' manes. Speechless they gazed at each other, eyes troubled, though in Hardin's gray eyes was a steely glint that held a promise of death.

Gage Hardin loomed almost grotesque in his height—he measured six feet and three inches in his bare feet—and astride his horse he towered skyward. He was an impressive figure of a man whose skin was burned to an Indian bronze by the sun and hot winds, nights and days of riding range. Under his smooth skin, muscles that outdoor life had built rippled silkily, giving an impression of strength in leash.

Doe Gaston commanded a bare five feet and ten inches booted, but he was so blockily built that he seemed a full two inches shorter than he was. His freckled face was one that was made for rollicking laughter, but now it was grim, the lines of his mouth drawn in with pain at the knowledge of how the story he had just told had hurt the tall man who faced him. As if repeating a sorely learned lesson he said again what had brought him.

"There was nothing else to do—so I came for you, secretly. Nobody has an idea I've left the ranch." Gaston's heavy shoulders moved slightly in a helpless shrug. "No one would be looking for either of us here where Tammer Canyon ends and the desert begins, and I knew you'd be going this way. I knew if anything was to be done to straighten things out that it wouldn't do for that buzzard bunch to realize you had word—yet."

"I would expect you to do the wise thing, Doe," Hardin said, his voice cold and hard as the stones beside the trail. "You always have—always will." The young rancher's gaze was inscrutable, intent on Doe Gaston's face, as though he believed not yet had the worst been told. He added dully: "How was he killed?"

He could not bring himself to say the name of Lonny Pope, the young waddy who for so long had been like a brother to him—Lonny, dead! Murdered! While watching out for the girl who meant more than life to Gage Hardin. It was beating over and over in his head with the insistence of a sharp pain: "Lonny dead—Mary gone!" His eyes were not even on Doe Gaston as he heard his partner answer:

"He was shot, Gage. His body and head showed seven bullet wounds. His hands—were tied behind his back."

Hardin drew in a raspy breath. "You saw him?" he asked.

"I found him, Gage," Gaston said in the same monotone.

"Dead?"

"Not quite. But he never regained consciousness. He

never said a word. Couldn't tell who—who—" The blocky man's lips tightened and his knuckles whitened where they rested on his cantle. "By God, if he only could have told, if we'd only had a thing to go on, I'd have—"

Gage Hardin raised one hand and passed it across his brow, as if he would wipe clear the frown that was not there, or erase the pictures that were dancing before his mind's eye.

"Where did you find him?" he asked. "Tell me everything you know, Doe. It's time for a showdown now!"

"Just inside the door of Mary Silver's cabin, Gage," Doe Gaston said, "like I told you. As soon as you lit out after Rood Vandover after that last killing of your horses, and you knew it *was* Rood, Lonny Pope took it in his head that maybe Mary needed to be watched.

"Lonny was wiser than we were, Gage, just because we've never been able to pin anything on Louis Peele and his gang, but it's simple enough now to see through the whole plot— hell—I'm not talking straight."

"I follow you, Doe," Hardin said grimly.

"They got you out of the way by making sure you would go after Vandover. Must be through with him to make him take it on the chin like that, but maybe he thought he could get clean away before you caught up with him. Anyhow, the minute you were gone, they went about their real business. They did enough damage to make certain you'd go after them the minute you got back. That's what they want! For some reason they want to get hold of *you* where they'll have you helpless in their hands. And for that reason Louis Peele has finally grown reckless, Gage."

"No argument there, Doe," he said dully. "He probably knew I was gone within an hour after I'd left Great Lost Valley, and got busy. Did—does anybody have any idea where Mary is? Where did she run off to?"

Doe Gaston's usually facile tongue stumbled, and he

turned his head as though he could not look into the eyes of his friend.

"Nobody knows," he mumbled.

Gage Hardin's great body jerked once, then stiffened to steeliness. One of his hands reached out to grip Gaston's shoulder in a rigid clasp.

"Doe!" he rasped. "What are you trying to tell me? You didn't say, at first, that they . . . I thought she had run away from them. . . . You don't mean that the way it sounds, do you?"

Gaston slowly nodded. "I'm afraid I do, Gage," he mumbled. "Louis and his gang—if they *were* the ones that killed Lonny, which I'd bet my life is so—took her with them when they went."

Gage Hardin dropped his hand as though it were suddenly leaden. His gaze was far away, and Doe Gaston could not be certain whether or not the moonlight alone caused his companion's face to appear a shade whiter. Never had the older partner seen the young rancher to whom he was so loyal show even so much as a trace of emotion. But he knew how this news he had brought had cut deep into Gage Hardin's soul until only blood payment could now atone.

A short dry laugh, without any trace of humor, a laugh that came from a heart filled with bitterness, cut shortly into the night air.

"Listen, Doe!" Hardin lowered his voice to say hurriedly, "I've got to talk fast. This is the time to save minutes now—and they're precious. I know what Louis Peele will do, as well as if he'd told me himself. He will find some quiet hiding place, and lie low there for a few days, waiting for me to track him and catch up with him, getting a nice little ambush all ready for me.

"He won't harm Mary. He knows he'll be walking right into the noose if he does. He's only taken the poor kid as bait for me—knowing I'd come after her hell-bent. Well,

I will! But first I've got to get Rood Vandover. I *have* to bring him back with me now, Doe. Everybody's suspected Rood was Louis' chief killer for some time, but it looks like Louis has shuffled him off now. Don't you see? That's my chance—the one I've waited for so long? I'll bring Rood Vandover back and turn him over to the law. The law—Guy Shawnessy—will make him talk all right, and furnish us with substantial evidence we might never get any other way.

"You go straight back to the Valley and tell the boys not to make a move until I get there at the ranch. I won't be twenty-four hours behind you."

"But Gage!" Gaston started to protest. "Vandover may be so far ahead of you that you'll never—"

Hardin cut him short. "He isn't," he snapped. "I know where he is. I haven't been trailing him this far for nothing. And I'll make sure of overtaking him in the shortest time possible. I've got a plan he won't guess." He straightened in the saddle and shrugged. "Get going, Doe," he said shortly.

For moments Gage Hardin sat motionless, watching his faithful friend fading into the cactus shadows. Behind him rugged mountains reared black and shapeless against the sky. Before him stretched the desert into which Rood Vandover had gone. Hardin's steely eyes narrowed to slits as for a moment he hesitated with the urge to gallop his horse out into that sandy waste, hell-bent after the man whom he meant to force to give him the revenge he had awaited for years. Then every muscle tightened as he shook off the temptation. He knew a better way. His plan—the one of which he had spoken—was sure fire. This was no time to take chances. He had to be *certain!* And as he had said, he knew where Vandover would be, just how far he could go in the time Hardin allotted himself for his own preparations.

"He'll have a surprise coming to him," he muttered, as

finally he turned his horse's head, when Gaston had passed from sight.

Promptly he headed back to the turn-off in the canyon that would lead him to rangeland and easier going, if it did take a little more time. It would be to his advantage in the long run.

He cast one glance back at the canyon mouth, out into the desert, just before he was out of sight of it. The moon shone down beneficently, and over all the desert nothing moved.

It was not rangeland going all the way for Gage Hardin though, as he urged his pony on with all speed possible. Soon he left it to skirt the foothills of the frowning mountains, at times moving through narrow forest trails so slight that only with great difficulty could he force a way through the growths of young spruce and scrub oak forming a tangled mass.

Before long, however, he dropped down over a rim and once more emerged on rangeland that was scrubby and sage-grown, far different from the rolling green acres on which his own cows fattened at the Circle Crossbar—when they were not brutally slaughtered or rustled.

It was the slaughtering that Gage Hardin could not understand. Rustling was all in a day's work. But too often of late he had found fine cattle killed, or wounded and left to die in agony. "Why?" had been the great, insistent question in his mind, but he was not even thinking of that now. More important questions had to be answered, and the pain in his heart left no room for material matters of business.

Bitterness filled him, but with it was a certain grim joy. At last had come to him the opportunity to pay a blood debt which only a promise had kept him from paying long ago. He was released from that now. Now he would be sure! As he had promised he would be. And siding him were some of the finest hell-roaring waddies that ever backed a man to the limit. Once he had Rood Vandover, and Shawnessy had forced Louis Peele's chief gunman to talk—

Hardin made swift time in the rough going, over scraggy land and through rock-strewn small arroyos, but the hours seemed to drag interminably, though he knew he was getting nearer and nearer his goal. Ahead now was another canyon leading onto the desert that would bring him out to his destination.

The night by now was swiftly passing, and gray beginning to steal over the land as the mountains grew blacker. The moon at last dropped down behind the horizon, leaving a misty aura to mark its passing behind the craggy tops. The shadows in the draws and coulees that had been purplish in the moonlight turned to black wells of menacing ebon.

Only the half glow of the false dawn, a faded violet, lighted the land and the desert seen faintly beyond as one by one the stars began to wink out in the great velvet canopy overhead. It, too, was changing, turning from midnight blue to a dirty gray, streaked with promise of a rising sun.

Hardin felt he had been traveling for days and nights when at last he rode through the final dark canyon and topped a small rise just beyond it. Looking ahead, he could see the desert plainly now, but nodded as the gray clumps of buildings rose up before it.

He touched his tired horse lightly, though his urge was to gallop at full tilt.

"Just a few more minutes now, boy," he muttered to his weary mount. "Rest then. We're almost there."

As though he understood, the horse whinnied lightly, and tossed his head. And as though he also understood the urge for speed in the man who bestrode him, he broke into a canter, headed for the dark clumps of buildings beyond.

"Surprise," Gage Hardin was muttering through his teeth. "Surprise for you, Rood Vandover—pronto!"

CHAPTER II

A DESERT-BRED HORSE

TEN minutes later, approaching the buildings in the graying morning, Gage Hardin crossed sun-baked land and over a rocky terrain so burned from the shimmer of the desert heat that even the yuccas and the stunted junipers appeared rocks themselves. And the nearer he came to his destination the harder his heart grew within him, the greater his determination.

All through his ride he had tried with might and main to put thoughts of Lonny Pope from him, but the picture of the laughing-eyed waddy persisted. He could hear his voice as he had so often heard it, raised in some lilt of the range. And Mary—

Mary's cabin—he could see it. Made of logs that kept out the heat of summer and the cold of winter. The corral, just big enough for her few head of horses, the hitch-rack outside her gate, the little flower garden she had made; and the trees through which the sun streamed in the spring and summer, and which could sparkle so with frost in the winter when all was warm and cozy inside. The small living room she had made home, where they always sat together before the red-hot pot-bellied stove, dreaming their dreams of the days to come, while he held her hand.

He could see that room as plainly as though it were thrown on a screen before him. Friendly, low-ceilinged, speaking so eloquently of a woman's touch, with the geraniums in the windows, the snowy white curtains. Somewhere Mary had got hold of a buffalo robe which she used for a rug—and how he used to laugh at her because she had hung flint-lock guns and rifles on her walls. And Indian blankets. She

14

had said it was the touch of the frontier, since she had come out here to make it her home and meant always to be a ranch girl.

The thoughts were bittersweet to Gage Hardin. How much they had planned, and now . . . Where was Mary now? Mary with her corn-silk hair, her cheeks like ocatilla blooms, her eyes like the sky at morning—

With such pictures before his mind's eye, it seemed an eternity before Hardin could traverse the space to the buildings sprawled at the edge of the desert. In fact it was less than thirty minutes. Hardin had made good time, far better time than had he headed straight into the desert. And this way he would have a chance.

Riding straight to the largest of the buildings, the ranch house, he dismounted and left his sweat-lathered, hard-ridden horse standing ground-hitched in the yard. Spurs jingling, he strode up to the front of the house, climbed the porch steps and knocked on the front door.

A third knock was necessary to bring response from within and his impatience grew. He was again lifting his fist for a thunderous pounding when he at last heard someone stir, then saw a light appear in a window at his left, obviously a bedroom. He watched the light being lifted and borne from room to room until it shone finally through the window beside the door at which he had knocked.

There was a rattling of a bar inside, then the door opened. It disclosed an elderly man with a short gray beard and a long gray night shirt that flapped around spindled legs. The gray man held the lamp high and peered outward with sharp gray eyes that gleamed under jutting, bushy gray eyebrows.

A gleam of approval came into the keen eyes, though, as he sized up Gage Hardin; a look that held a certain amount of admiration as he took in Hardin's big, broad-shouldered form, his six feet three of height, his inscrutable steely eyes and the sweep of dark hair beneath the dusty sombrero.

There was no mistaking Hardin's brand and earmarks to any man of the range, either desert or mountain-bred. He was a range rider of the top-hand brand, saddle-marked and weather-hardened, sun-browned and toughened until sinews were whipcord. A man who could take care of himself in any spot, but whom any well-meaning hombre need never fear.

"How jer do," the old man said, in a voice that quavered a little, though in spite of his age it was plain that he was strong and range-hardened himself. The gray eyes continued to sweep Hardin with a penetrating scrutiny of inquiry. "What can I do for you this time o' night—or mebbe I should say mornin'. Ain't lost on the desert, are ye?"

"No, I'm not lost," Hardin said quickly. "But I'd like to speak to you, if you don't mind. Hope you'll excuse me bustin' in so early like this. You're Mr. Hoaley, aren't you?"

"Correct." The old man nodded his shaggy head. "Shark Hoaley. Guess everybody knows me all right. The one man fool enough to run horses on this desert. Was you looking for me? If you was, you've come to the right place. Come on in and rest yourself while I find some pants."

Gage Hardin shook his head. "No, thanks," he said. "I'm in kind of a hurry. Yes, you're the man I was looking for. So I'll come right down to business here. I want to rent a desert-bred horse."

"*Rent* one?" The heavy brows were raised in amazement. "Who ever heard tell of the like! I reckon you had better come in a minute."

Hardin shrugged and stepped into the room, which proved to be a combination kitchen and living room. Hoaley set the lamp down on the nearby kitchen table and turned to survey Hardin with a frown. It was as if he were revising his first quick scrutiny of the young rancher.

"I don't rent horses," the old man said tersely. "I run 'em

and sell 'em. But you can borrow one if you've got any real good use for it, and can tell me what it is and who you are."

"I'll explain as much as I can," the tall young rancher said, with a touch of growing impatience. "It's for you to judge how badly I need one of your horses and whether I can have it or not. I am Gage Hardin, from Great Lost Valley, in the mountains to the north. I guess you know the place. It's an isolated district, only a few ranches there; only four of 'em to be exact. All of us have been annoyed for some time by a group of badmen who have moved in among us, bandits and rustlers who have been posing as honest cattlemen, and have been using their own ranch as a base of operations.

"They've been mostly giving their attention to me and my Circle Crossbar spread. They have set fire to my haystacks, poisoned what water springs they could, and that isn't half. Last thing they've done is to butcher my cattle instead of rustling them, and now a day or two ago, they ran off and butchered my best drove of saddle-stock breeders. At least one of their outfit did—and then he got out of the Valley in a hurry. I had plenty of proof, from the boys of my own outfit who saw it, without being near enough to do anything about it, so I hightailed after the horse butcher.

"I trailed him to this desert. Less than an hour ago my partner in the Crossbar overtook me, to tell me that this same outfit had just killed one of my best men—a young bucko I looked on as a brother—and had taken the girl I am going to marry. Naturally I have to return with all possible speed to attend to that matter, as you can see, and more than ever I've got to take back with me the man I've come to get. I haven't caught sight of him yet, but I've gone far enough to know he's headed for the Devil's Dance Floor—and he's on a mountain-bred horse!"

"That's enough," old Hoaley said, cutting in before Gage

Hardin could say any more. "I reckon I know why you want a desert-bred horse now. That's the only kind I've got. Come along."

The old man had been slipping into some clothes and pulling on boots as Hardin talked. Now he motioned to the rancher and Hardin followed him out of the house through the back door. From a peg on the wall just outside the kitchen door, Hoaley took down a lantern, lighted it, and led the way toward the barn.

Halfway across the yard, he turned as he saw the bulk of Hardin's winded horse standing ground-hitched, and stopped a second, motioning toward it.

"That your mount there?" he asked, then chortled a little. "Asking fool question, ain't I? I suppose it must be. I didn't leave none there my ownself."

"Yes, that's mine," Hardin told him. "Chaser, his name is. My own best mount. One of the finest horses bred in the mountains. And one of the fastest—on hard ground. But on desert sand, and tired as he is—"

"You reckon this fellow you're chasin' wouldn't have had time to stop and get a desert-bred horse for himself anywhere?" the old man asked quickly but Hardin shook his head.

"It would scarcely be a matter of time," he said, "though I'm pretty sure he hasn't had such a chance." He paused, waiting for Hoaley to slide back the ponderous door. "It's a matter of ignorance with him, Mr. Hoaley. He doesn't know what hard riding through the desert can do to a mountain horse. He's always lived in the mountains—and his one idea right now is to get away as quick as he can, which he thinks he can do because he's on a good fast horse.

"Anyway, I don't believe he knows just what he is up against or what I'll do when I find him, because he doesn't know, as I know now, that he has been made to look responsible for everything by others who think they'll get away with anything after I've found this one. All he knows is that he was told to get me as far away from home as possible, and maybe he doesn't even know why—as I told you—because he doesn't know what's happened in the Valley since he left there after butchering my horses. The main thing now is that I'm the one who has to make speed."

"Well, we'll see that you make it," the old man promised grimly.

He stepped into the barn and Hardin followed him. Old Hoaley walked on a short distance in the silence that was broken only by the restless stamping of the hoofs of stalled horses disturbed. He stopped, reached up and hung the lantern on a nail driven into the wall a couple of feet above his head. It threw a dim yellow glow over the barn floor and the stalls.

"Your man," he said to Hardin, "is headed for a bad break if he doesn't want you to catch him, riding into the Devil's Dance Floor on a mountain horse that's already done a heap of traveling, if I get you right. That's the meanest piece of desert in this part of the country, Hardin, and I reckon I know 'em all. But don't let that bother you . . . See this old plug here?" He gestured toward a stall opposite the spot where he and Hardin were standing. "His name's Scotch. Maybe you don't think he's much on looks, but him and the desert are blood brothers, I'm thinking."

In the stall was a horse that at a glance Gage Hardin could see was as notably bred to the desert as Chaser had been bred to the hills. Where Chaser was long and thin, lean in flank and wide in barrel, Scotch was thick-muscled, round-bodied, deep in the barrel. Where Chaser's hoofs were high, definitely ovate, habituated to rock, hard ground and steep slopes which he could climb like a mountain goat, Scotch's hoofs were wide-splayed, almost as round as a plate, fashioned by habit to combat shifting sand. Through them he could drift along as a man on snow-shoes travels along the hard or soft-piled snow.

"Scotch will take you to the Devil's Dance Floor, Hardin," Hoaley said. "He'll see you through any desert ever made, and be ready to start all over again when you get where you're going."

He reached for a saddle hanging on the wall, but Gage Hardin quickly interposed:

"Never mind. I have my own saddle."

Hoaley grinned toothlessly. "Hmmph!" he snorted. "I was beginning to think you knew the desert. But you don't know it so damn well, hey? That big stock saddle of yours is too heavy for desert going, man. You have to travel light when you're hitting it across the sands. Now you listen here. If you want to make time, I'll fit you out and see that you make it. Just you leave it all to me. First thing—take off them heavy woollies. You don't want them kind of chaps here. This here is what we wear on the desert. While I'm saddling up, get into 'em, son."

From the wall a little way beyond he took down a pair of heavy bullhide "chinks." Desert chaps. In general construction they were much like the ordinary chaps to which Gage Hardin was accustomed, belted at the waist like other chaparajos. But they were cut in much narrower lines and, containing no back piece, were held in place along thigh and shin by the straps fitted across the back of the leg. Hoaley tossed them to Hardin.

"Put 'em on," he repeated. "You'll right soon find out why. They're lighter, you understand." The old man removed a bridle from another peg as he spoke. "They protect your legs from the cactus better. Them woollies would get all snarled up in them stickers before you could say Jack Robinson."

·Just twenty-one minutes from the time he had rapped at Hoaley's front door, Hardin stood in the yard at the side of

the docile, saddled and bridled Scotch. Chaser was already
in a stall in the barn, busy with a much needed feeding, and
with Hoaley's promise of a rub-down. Hoaley was standing
at Scotch's head now, as Hardin swung into the unfamiliar
saddle.

"I'm leaving Chaser and my rig here as security, Mr.
Hoaley," he told the old horse runner. "If I don't make it
back, he's yours. If I do come back, I'll pay you for the use
of Scotch."

"I want no pay of any sort," Hoaley snorted, and retreated
a pace from the horse's head, glaring up at the tall rider.
"You just come back, that's all. That's pay enough. And
remember there's no water fit to drink anywhere on that
desert! You will have to make them canteens I gave you
last you there and back—wherever you catch up with your
lobo. Be sparing of the water yourself, and don't give
Scotch much. He ain't used to it. Just give him enough to
keep him going. Laws, sometimes I begin to think that little
horse's ma must have been some kin to a camel!"

"I'll remember," Hardin promised grimly, though fully
realizing that the old man's words were meant to cheer him
up on his journey. "Well, good night, Mr. Hoaley. Maybe
I can do something in return some day. You've just got to
call on me."

"Good night, son." Hoaley took one swift step toward
the mounted man and laid a hand on the bridle rein.
"Listen, Gage Hardin. I'm an old man, and maybe I've seen
a few things in the world you haven't had a chance to learn
yet. But there's one thing: I have always held that a man
who was afraid to throw in his last chip was a mighty poor
gambler. Anyways when everything else he's got is in the
pot. And we're all gamblers, Hardin—one way or another,
though maybe some of us kind of hesitate to admit it. The
fellows who buck the game hard enough—all the way

through—are the ones that win. That's all. I'll be seeing you."

The roan stretched his legs and threw out his big splayed feet. The sand showered behind him. Man and horse were gone, down the face of the desert—

To those who are not worthy of her favors and who cross her grim borders, the desert ruthlessly and relentlessly deals death, for there is no patience in her soul for either weaklings or those who will not stop to learn her moods and cater to her whims. But to those few who love her, she can give with tenderness and generosity. To such men—men like old Shark Hoaley, she can give of her rich secrets, her beauty, and sometimes the gold that men hold dear.

And so was Gage Hardin girded as he set out on his quest, by the advice of a man who knew and had traveled his desert, who loved it. Men might have called Shark Hoaley a desert rat, but that would have been because they did not know. In fact, he was one of the world's strong, who had learned from Nature, who had learned to live alone, by his own strength. And it was the feeling of that added strength that was in Gage Hardin's veins as he set out grimly through forests of gaunt cacti, through rolling dune wastes, weirdly sculptured in the dawning day.

Soon there would be a brassy glare that would burn his eyeballs—he knew it. Heat waves would billow up stiflingly. Deep sand would try to ensnare even Scotch's splayed hoofs.

But none of it mattered. His eyes were set straight ahead. And in his heart was one grim purpose—to catch Rood Vandover and bring him back, thereby bringing nearer the justice for which he had vainly fought for nine years.

CHAPTER III

GAGE HARDIN and Scotch were still traveling steadily long after the gray of dawn had given way to tenuous fingers of crimson and crystal light that slanted across the desert sands, turning them to shimmering gold. The sun, as it rose with startling suddenness over the horizon, poured a quivering sea of molten brass over the waste of sand and cactus and yucca, touching here and there a huge boulder that rose menacingly out of the yellow ocean.

Hardin sat loosely in the saddle, forcing the horse to an even mile-annihilating pace, though his every instinct was for spur and galloping haste. Scotch lived up to his owner's praise of him. The horse seemed to know the desert, as he knew the potency of his own spread hoofs.

Gage Hardin smiled just once on that ride, and that was when for an instant he did manage to force his mind away from Lonny Pope and Mary and his own grim purpose. He smiled in remembrance of a story he had heard told in the bunkhouse. This ride of his was remindful of it. The story, as he recalled it, concerned a man in urgent need of making an extended ride, a man who passed a boy riding in the same direction and sought information of him.

Drawing abreast of the boy, so the bunkhouse rannies had told it, the man had inquired: "Say, boy, do you think I can make it to town by sunset?"

The boy surveyed the man's mount calculatingly, and answered in a drawl: "Yeah. If you ride slow enough."

The man scowled and rode on, forcing his horse to the utmost. Some hours later he was obliged to slow his weary mount to a mere persistent plodding. The boy came canter-

ing by on an eager, still-fresh horse. The man, anxious and
perturbed, called to him again: "Say, boy! Can I make it
to town by sunset?"

And the boy, glancing back over his shoulder, answered
curtly: "Yeah. If you ride fast enough."

Hardin was taking no chances. He saw to it that the roan
Scotch traveled slowly enough. There might be need for
speed later—all that the stout-hearted little desert horse
could give. Several times he halted the animal, to swab the
dust and sand from Scotch's nostrils with a wet bandanna,
and to give him a mere sip of water from one of the canteens.

What old Hoaley had said was true. Hardin did not know
the desert. He knew of it only, and had been glad enough
of the old man's advice. But he did know horses, he knew
how to treat them, and how to ride. He knew the steady,
patient method of putting the miles behind him, which was
not much different in the sand with the proper horse under
him than long miles ridden over hard ground.

At last, when the sun was climbing steadily toward the
meridian, and the heat waves were like oven blasts, Hardin
saw dimly, through the shimmering hot air, due ahead, the
low-lying arc of dunes that rimmed the Devil's Dance Floor.
Though he had never been here before, Hardin recognized
the approach to the Devil's Dance Floor immediately, for
Hoaley had impressed the dune formation upon him as an
unmistakable landmark of his destination.

Pulling Scotch to a halt, Hardin sat motionless on the
panting animal's back, his hands crossed on the saddle horn,
keenly studying the forbidding country spread before him,
and searching for signs of his quarry. This was a kind of
country with which he, used to rolling green prairie and
lush-topped mesa land, was unfamiliar.

It was a country which he viewed with vast repugnance
and unease, though he had realized he was coming to the
open door of hell, as he had heard it described. It was a

kind of nightmare country, a place of shifting sand held in place for the time being by low, matted patches of cacti and dry, unpleasant weeds the names of which he did not even know. And all of it looked as if it might shift at any moment to let the unsuspecting slip down into still hotter nether regions.

The only alternate sign of living growth was the aborted shapes of taller cacti, grotesque, contorted forms, like shambling skeletons stationed there by the desert itself as a grim warning to man not to enter.

Hardin's gaze dropped to the sands. A few yards to his right were the clear tracks of Rood Vandover's horse. He had followed them long enough and steadily enough for the past two days to be certain of them. As he had supposed, his quarry could not be far ahead of him, taking this quickest, if most terrible way of getting across the desert.

"Get along, Scotch," Hardin said tersely to the desert horse.

Head hanging, with his nose close to the sand, Scotch moved on at a swinging walk, his course directly toward the heaving dunes as though he sensed their destination. In less than three-quarters of an hour, at that steady pace, Hardin arrived at and passed the sand hills spread in an arc around the approach to the awesome Devil's Dance Floor.

Before him there burst into sight a vast level sweep of desert over which the sun beat down with a molten glare. But he gave it only one sweeping glance as he caught his breath in an involuntary ejaculation of gratified triumph. For not more than half a mile distant Rood Vandover plodded ahead on his black horse at a dogged walk!

Gage Hardin frowned, thinking swiftly. Of course Vandover had expected to be followed, had hoped to pull Hardin away from Great Lost Valley; though equally of course he had thought eventually to escape his pursuer. Apparently now Vandover had no idea that it would have been possible for Hardin to have drawn so close.

Hardin drew himself erect. The time for speed was now! Just one-half mile more, and—

He settled low in his saddle and touched Scotch lightly with his spurs. Not even in such an emergency would he rowel any horse. But even at the light touch Scotch responded so swiftly that Hardin's hat swept from his head in the sudden rush of hot air, hanging down his back by its strap. He grabbed at it, swiftly clapping it back onto his head as the sun seemed to burn straight through his scalp.

Hardin's thin, sweat-reeked shirt slapped against his skin as the horse made swift, bounding over the sand. The splayed hoofs of the desert-bred horse lashed the flying white particles into a spray that swept past Gage Hardin's bandanna-protected mouth and nose. In that abrupt burst of speed, as the unsuspecting Vandover still jogged onward at his leisurely pace, unaware of vengeance flying at him, Hardin cut down the distance between himself and the fugitive man and horse by a good half.

Then, as if touched by some prescience of danger, Rood Vandover turned in his saddle and glanced uneasily rearward. As if stung by a thong of rawhide he straightened from his lounging attitude, whipping up his long-lashed quirt and bringing it furiously down on the flank of the exhausted black horse.

The big black reared and leaped forward, plunging into a wild gallop. For a short space, pursued and pursuer drew noticeably apart across the shifting sands, but after the initial fruitless dash they settled down to a punishing steady pace in which neither of them gained. Leaping over small clumps of cacti, darting around larger masses, weaving in and out between huge barrel cacti that reared their spiny growth skyward, with manes and tails flying the two horses bore their riders at a terrific pace over the face of the desert, oblivious to everything but their race. Even the sun that seared like scorching flame into sweat-flecked bodies was forgotten.

It was apparent that Vandover, after that first flash of dismay, had lapsed into a period of reassurance. He knew that he was riding a phenomenally fast horse and the one glance that he had caught of Gage Hardin's horse had added to his reassurance. But now he was thinking more of escape than he was thinking of the way of escape. He began to grow anxious as he saw he was not gaining. And his confidence in his ability to elude the man behind him was short-lived.

Escape began quickly to seem less certain, as he realized that his black could not long maintain this deadly pace. Swept by his first real fear of being overtaken, Rood Vandover made the error that Hardin had half expected him to make. He began to beat his tiring horse without mercy, striving to force the spent animal to greater speed, a thing beyond the capacity of horseflesh.

The black gelding was already given the best that was in its great sturdy heart. But the roan was trained for such desert pursuit. Scotch began to gain. And Gage Hardin's lips tightened to a grim straight line as he saw the quivering of the black horse ahead as the cruel quirt lashed down again and again.

That anything living could maintain such a galling pace under such conditions was beyond possibility. The bodies of the two horses were white-lathered with sweat. Their feet lashed with such speed in the maelstrom of flying sand that their speeding legs were a blur. Their breathing was a painful shriek through expanded nostrils in which stinging white particles lodged. Flecks of foam blew from their mouths upon their breasts and upon their riders' clothes.

Both men knew that the harsh battle of pace could last little longer. But Rood Vandover knew it the better of the two. His faint-born fear rose to panic. He had not bargained for his nemesis to reach him here in the heart of the blistering desert where there were none of his gun companions to come to his aid. And his one hope—the swift horse upon which he had depended—was fast failing him.

The black horse was laboring hideously, but could gain nothing over the relentlessly pursuing roan. Instead, the gap between the two horses steadily diminished—to four hundred yards; to three hundred.

Then it was that Vandover's courage failed him completely. Snatching his rifle from his saddle boot, he twisted about in the saddle, and with a last desperate effort at defense, began firing backward. His aim was shaken by the racing horse and the shimmering of the heat waves. Besides, he was too badly crazed by his fear of Gage Hardin's righteous rage to think sanely.

CHAPTER IV

VANDOVER'S DEFIANCE

AT THE first report of the rifle, Hardin straightened in his saddle. He raised himself in his stirrups and issued a sharp word of command to the roan. Scotch had a reserve of speed remaining—something of which Hardin had been certain, and upon which he had banked for the showdown.

The gap between the two horses diminished. It lessened to a mere hundred yards.

Vandover shouted a rasping, despairing curse. The rifle had been emptied of its last shell and none of his shots had come close to the man who was so swiftly gaining on him. With a yell of defiance he flung the rifle far out into the sand and reached for the revolver at his belt.

But before he could even get it out of its holster, the black horse's straining pace took its toll. The spent horse, blinded by the sweat and dust and sand particles filming his eyes, tortured by the effort of his laboring lungs, struck an upstanding rock in the treacherous sand. The black lunged madly and went down, floundering, striking the floor of the desert with a crash, describing a complete somersault that threw the rider several feet beyond in a sprawling heap.

Hardin reined the panting Scotch to a halt within a few yards of the prone black horse and leaped to the ground. The black lay utterly still, mouth open, tongue lolling to the sand, barrel heaving painfully, eyes rolling in agony. Hardin's gaze focused on the distortion of the slender forelegs of the well-bred animal. Both of them had been broken by the punishing fall.

Rood Vandover struggled frantically to his feet, momentarily stunned by the crash, and stood staring stupidly

29

at Gage Hardin. But he made no further attempt to go for his holstered gun, for Hardin's own gun muzzle was boring at him steadily. With colossal difficulty the downed gunman found his voice.

"I was hoping"—he made an attempt to wet dry lips with a dry, quivering tongue as he rasped out his lie—"I was hoping that you would not come after me, Gage, when you found—found . . . For your own sake—'cause you was more needed in the Valley. Believe me or not, I was hoping you wouldn't come! I—I hated to do that to your—horses. But I had to. Louis made me do it! It—it was all part of a trap to get you away."

"You are telling me nothing." Hardin held Rood Vandover's gaze with eyes that concealed his bitterness, and his tone held the coldness of judgment. "None of your excuses matter now, Rood. I am taking you back to answer charges. You have done Louis Peele's bidding just once too often, Vandover. I could kill you now—but I'm taking you back to the law."

"Taking me back, Gage? Not me! I killed your horses, yes. It's no use trying to deny that, for it was planned for you to know it was me. But I killed them because Louis made me. It was all part of a trap, I tell you, and I'll admit I even helped plan that—how to get you away from the Valley while Louis did something else he wanted to do. He didn't tell me what—that's Gawd's truth! And take it or leave it, everything I did was because it was the only way I saw of getting clear of Louis Peele. And now that I've *got* clear of the sidewinder who had me, body and soul, I'm not going back! Not for you or any other man wearing shoe leather!"

"You are going back, Rood," Hardin replied quietly, his voice the same monotone of deadly accusation. "You are—"

"Listen to me, Gage!" Vandover pleaded desperately, his face colorless beneath the sun's burning, his eyes despairing. "I'll make a bargain with you. Listen! What would you give to know what became of your brother Bruce, back there where you lived before—the Valley?"

Hardin drew a deep, hard breath, but his eyes held steadily, inexorably on the cringing gunman.

"Nothing, Rood," he said coldly. "I have known for nearly nine years that my brother was dead."

Vandover laughed, a strange, insane sound in the desert air.

"Oh, yes, he's dead all right. But—wouldn't you give a good deal to know *how* he died? You never did know, did you? And ever since you'd have given your right arm to know how—and why, and who. You know you would—and so do I. You may *suspect,* but you'd give something to *know.* Fair enough. I do know. And so I'm making you a proposition. You let me get away, let me go on into Mexico—I swear you nor nobody else in the Valley will ever hear of me again—and I'll give you enough on Louis Peele to—"

"I have enough on Louis Peele now to hang him to the highest tree, Rood," Hardin said, his voice icily cold, hard. "I make no bargains with a treacherous rat like you. You are going back with me, so stop trying to argue, and do as I say. I have enough water to see us back across the desert. We will take turns walking, and riding my horse." Again his lips tightened, as he shot a quick glance at the suffering animal in the sand. "But the first thing you are to do is to walk over there and shoot that black horse of yours."

"Shoot him yourself!" snapped Vandover, but a queer gleam came into his eyes that Gage Hardin did not miss.

"And give you a chance to draw on me?" sneered Hardin.

Vandover slumped, defeated, his eyes on the gun held so steadily in the tall young rancher's hand.

"Turn your back to me," commanded Hardin. "Now draw your gun and shoot the horse. Then throw your gun behind you and stay where you are until I get the gun."

Vandover tried to straighten, as within him despair and terror won all odds, but his shoulders would not entirely come out of their slump. Even though his back was turned he knew that he would have no chance, even with a gun in his hand, for Hardin's own gun was unswervingly between his shoulder blades. He would be a dead man before he could even whirl with his own weapon.

Slowly he drew his gun from its holster—the weapon so useless now for his own purpose. As steadily as he could, he aimed it at the head of the black horse, and with neat precision put a bullet through the animal's brain. The horse quivered once, kicked feebly with its hind feet, and again lay still.

"Now toss that gun behind you," came Hardin's calm monotone, and the gun plumped into the sand a few feet beyond the tall rancher.

But Gage Hardin was not prepared for Rood Vandover's next swift move, perhaps because he had not fully realized the depths of despair in the man's black heart. He had not thought that Vandover would whirl to make battle, weapon-less, in the face of a covering gun. But that was exactly what the gunman did!

Before he could actually grasp the fact that it was coming, Hardin saw a big fist flash at his chin as Rood Vandover whirled, lightninglike, cursing and staggering, but filled with the courage of despair. With an instinctive roll of his head Hardin evaded the punch, but before he could get his gun into action, the brutishly husky man was on him, closing in so that gun play was impossible. One of Vandover's hands was grasping the rancher's wrist in a viselike grip, and with the other huge hand he was reaching for Hardin's throat, the thick, steely fingers kinked like talons.

Gage Hardin knew Vandover of old, knew his reputation in a rough-and-tumble fight; knew especially now, with so much at stake, that he would use everything. He also knew the man's strength and knew that if those devilish hands once found his windpipe that it would be quickly crushed.

Thinking quickly, knowing that for the moment the gun in the hand that Vandover gripped would be useless, Hardin hooked up his left fist in a hard uppercut aimed at Vandover's apelike jaw. But the bunched knuckles did not connect, for Vandover jerked his head aside at just the right moment, and Hardin's fist smashed solidly on the gunman's nose. He felt the impact along his own arm as he also felt bone and cartilage crunch. Vandover let out a bull roar and shook his head as the blood spattered.

"I'll kill you for that!" he howled. "I wasn't going to, but now—"

Raging like an angry bull, Vandover hurled the full strength of his body against Hardin, trying to fling him to the sand. He was still holding the rancher's gun hand rigid, but was swinging his huge fist at Hardin's head with a rage that was accentuated by the pain of his crushed nose.

But even as that hamlike fist drove, Hardin ducked, then quickly straightened as again his own fist slashed out. It was an awkward position from which to hurl a killing blow, but somehow Gage Hardin managed it. It was a punch that started somewhere from down at his knees and gathered strength along the way until it landed like a flaming meteor on Rood Vandover's jaw.

It landed properly that time, too. Hardin could feel it himself, all the way from his connecting fist along his arm, and down through his body as it landed on Vandover's jaw with a sound like that of a meat cleaver hitting a side of beef. But the next instant he saw the hairy face that had been so close to his retreat as Vandover's head snapped backward. Then he felt the death grip on his gun hand loosen, saw his antagonist, with a dazed expression in his eyes, slumped backward to the sand as his knees buckled.

Hardin's gun was held steadily on the man who had made his final desperate play for freedom. Rood Vandover struggled to his knees and knelt there a moment, head hanging, as he shook it groggily.

"Get up, Rood," Hardin said grimly. "It's no use. I told you that you were going back."

Vandover glanced up at him—once—through bleared eyes.

"I told you I wasn't going back—to Louis Peele," he mumbled. "I meant it."

Gage Hardin had thought his antagonist's last play had been made, and was not prepared for any further resistance. In the heat of the fight, he had completely forgotten the gun that Vandover had tossed behind him at the rancher's orders. But Vandover had not forgotten it. He had been reminded of it when he had fallen flat on the hard metal of the six-gun. But he knew he would never get a chance to use it on Gage Hardin who stood there so coldly merciless, with his own gun muzzle aimed straight at Vandover's heart.

After that all but knock-out blow, Hardin would not have believed Rood Vandover could move so fast as he did then. But the next instant, he saw the man's hand go slightly behind him, saw the glitter of the weapon in a movement so swift it was a blur in the blistering sunlight. As though it were all the same blurring movement, Vandover whipped the gun to his own temple and fired.

Hardin averted his face as Vandover went down into the sand again—never again to rise, this time. The act had been so unexpected, its results were so irrevocably final that for the moment he felt stunned, nauseated. For so swiftly did it happen that Rood Vandover was dead before he struck the sand.

At last he had hurled his defiance in Hardin's face—a defiance that could not be denied. He was not going back to Louis Peele.

CHAPTER V

HARDIN'S RETURN

FOUR days later, in that dusk which lies between sunset and moonrise, and all the rangeland lies in quiet dreaming, Doe Gaston heard a familiar step on the back stairs. Gaston had gone to bed early, weary with his conjectures about what could have happened to Gage Hardin, as well as about what was still to come. But he had not yet gone to sleep.

Gaston turned and lighted the lamp on the table against the wall, as Hardin closed the door, came in and slumped down into a chair before he spoke. His shoulders spoke eloquently of a mission that had not been accomplished, before Gaston said a word.

From the blackness of the yard there came the faint nicker of a horse. Chaser knew he was home. He was wondering why he had been left there, still saddled and bridled, with his comfortable stall so near.

"I thought—" Gaston expended his breath in a gust, as the lamplight grew from the ignited wick and steadied. "I thought you were never coming. Where is Vandover? Couldn't you find him?"

"I didn't bring him, after all," Hardin said dully.

He slipped deeper down into his chair, his attention seemingly focused on the table and the lighted lamp. He did not look at Gaston as he suddenly began talking and hastily recounted all that had happened, in minute detail, since he and Gaston had parted there at the edge of the desert.

"He shot himself before I could make a move to stop him. I had to bury him there on the desert. I didn't dare try to bring him back all that distance in the hot sun, with only one horse. It really doesn't matter, anyway, Doe. I took Scotch back to Hoaley. He wouldn't accept anything for the use of him. I got Chaser—and here I am. What has been happening around here?"

Gaston huddled in his underwear. "Nothing has had much time to develop, Gage. But I did this—I sent Red Corcoran for Sheriff Shawnessy. When the sheriff got here, I simply told him to go find Mary Silver."

Hardin nodded, staring at the wall, in blank silence. His mind traveled back to the time when he had first come to Great Lost Valley, eight years before, when Guy Shawnessy had just been elected sheriff of Grant County. Great Lost Valley had then been wild and unsettled country.

Hardin had arrived in it with money enough at hand to buy the acres encompassing most of the rich valley and a great deal of the excellent rangeland to the south and west of it. He had established at that time the Circle Crossbar Ranch.

Within three years other families had moved into the Valley, and ranches had grown up around him to the east and north. Fred Warde had come with his wife and two sons, Gilbert and Lester, to found the Diamond W Ranch. Jefferson Baker, with his wife and three sons, Toby, Ferris and Walt, and his infant daughter Annie, had founded the J Bar B Ranch.

Not long after that, less than a year of time, Hardin had met Doc Gaston in Heppner, and Doc had eventually accepted a place as partner of the Circle Crossbar. A strange and unaccountable loneliness, but a loneliness nevertheless forever manifest, had lingered about Gage Hardin. Doc had never succeeded either in banishing it or sounding it.

The next people to move into the Valley, five years after Hardin's advent, had been Mary Silver and her elder brother Melvin. Mel was apparently dying on his feet, of a treacherous heart, and he had wanted to die in the mountains.

Brother and sister had purchased a patch of land a few

miles up the Valley from the Circle Crossbar, and had settled to make a home. Mel had not died. He had grown strong and secure.

Guy Shawnessy and Gage Hardin had realized in the same week that they both loved Mary Silver. She had had eyes only for Hardin, and she was of too honest fiber to make any pretense otherwise.

Shawnessy, needing but little and showing himself seldom in that territory, had taken his loss with grace—but he had never forgotten that he loved Mary Silver. Neither had Gage Hardin forgotten.

Gage stirred in his chair, bleak gaze intent on Doe Gaston. "You sent for Guy?"

"I did." Doe pulled his long-sleeved underwear over his wrists. "I figured that if there was one man besides you who would turn the world over to find Mary he would be Guy Shawnessy. He asked for a posse of picked men. I gave him Red Corcoran, Dutch Sundquist, Tamm Oaks, and Salt River Charley. They left yesterday at sun-up. I waited here for you. I haven't much of a head for details, Gage. I did what I could."

"You did all any man could do." Hardin smiled, and this time it was not a grimace that he achieved. "You shot true, Doe. If Guy can't find her——" He left the sentence hanging, remembering the coming of Louis Peele to Great Lost Valley.

Peele had first shown himself in the Valley four years ago. He had quietly investigated the Valley, to be certain that he had found Gage Hardin at last, then had bought the last remaining stretch of land in the Valley, the tract lying to the south of the Circle Crossbar, between Hardin's ranch and the Diamond W.

From that day, Doe Gaston had known that old enmity existed between Gage Hardin and Louis Peele. The fact was blatantly evident in Peele's mock courtesy whenever he chanced to meet any members of the Circle Crossbar crew. It was quite as evident in Hardin's thin-lipped silence.

The more Doe had seen of Peele's outfit, the more uneasy he had become. Doe Gaston never asked questions, but he had done more than one man's share of wondering.

He had wondered why Hardin, with an inscrutable wry smile on his face, had nicknamed the cowboy inseparables, Corcoran, Sundquist, Oaks and Salt River Charley, the "Four from Hell's Hill." He had wondered why Hardin's ancient enemy should deliberately move into Great Lost Valley and settle next the Circle Crossbar. Doe's wondering had not decreased as time's cycles waxed and waned. Peele had grown increasingly nasty and belligerent with every year that passed. Seeing that his nastiness and belligerence did not draw Hardin's retaliation, Peele had begun to commit numerous depredations, such as cutting fences, stealing a few calves, butchering young beef, gradually growing bolder and more vindictive. And though those acts could never be proved to have been performed by Peele and his men, every hand on the Circle Crossbar knew that the guilt lay at their doors.

Doe's wondering had come to be almost unbearable. He had wondered why Hardin had sternly forbidden any of his crew to visit the least reprisal on Peele. Such an inactive course under persecution wasn't reasonable; but it prevailed rigidly under Hardin's strict orders. Hardin had said just once that he was waiting the day when Peele would break all moorings and commit some overt act, rendering himself irrevocably answerable to the law. Doe had wondered at that, too, but his inarticulate wondering had availed him nothing.

He sat now, huddled in his chair in his underclothing, staring at the returned Hardin, startled to note that that inscrutable wry smile was again on Gage Hardin's face.

"So." Hardin roused himself, and drew his big body erect. "So—you sent Guy Shawnessy to find Mary, and for posse you gave him—the Four from Hell's Hill!"

"Yes." Doe repressed a shiver; something emanating from Hardin chilled him.

Hardin's smile softened, relaxing a little. "It's all right, Doe. You couldn't have done a better thing. I—you——" The smile faded now. "You don't know much about me, do you, Doe? I've always meant to tell you when the time came. Well, it's come." He leaned forward in his chair, his eyes fixed intently on Gaston's face. "A long way from here, Doe, boy, in the high cattle country around—well, no matter: but a long way from here there is a mountain country that rises to its crown in a high peak. Back there they call that particular peak Hell's Hill. It is one solid, strange mass of red rock, queer stuff ranging all the way from deep red to bright brick color.

"Fifteen years ago, when I was a youngster of sixteen, there were two families growing up in that ranching country, near the town of Tenville: two families living side by side, the Hardins and the Peeles. There were two boys in each family, two only—Louis Peele and his brother Harry, my brother Bruce and myself. Bruce was nineteen years old then. Louis was twenty, and Harry was twenty-two. We four about lived together; we were with each other so much that the people living there nicknamed us the Four from Hell's Hill."

"Oh!" Doe Gaston started.

For a fleeting instant Hardin's thin smile returned. "Yes, Doe. That's where it all started. I'll try to get it said as short as possible. That friendship continued for about two years. Bruce and I were the younger, we were easily influenced.

"We thought Louis and Harry were fine fellows, reckless and full of the devil, but we didn't realize that they were bad. Not till my father warned Bruce and me. He said Louis and Harry had been getting themselves into some pretty wild scrapes, and if we didn't stay away from them they were going to get us into trouble. He was alarmed, and he succeeded in alarming us. We began to stay away from the Peeles.

"About that time Mrs. Peele died. Less than a month later my father was gored to death by a range steer. We made his death an excuse to stay at home, to keep quiet and avoid further truck with Louis and Harry. The Four from Hell's Hill were on the verge of a permanent break, and Louis didn't like it. I realize now that he wanted to use us, to make us his goats. He began prodding us and jeering at us, trying to force us to join them again. We tried to resist, but he had a smooth tongue.

"Louis pretended to see at last that he and Harry had been bad ones, and they promised to change—to act more like grown, honest folks—provided we two would take up our old ways with them again. Well, what would you expect, Doe? We'd been brought up together. We believed Louis.

"We hadn't more than begun to run around with them again, when Louis and Harry held up a pack train of mules traveling north with a fortune in cash. The pack train belonged to a couple of old prospectors who had made a fair strike, had carted their ore to town and converted it into cash. They were on the way home with their money, all in one-thousand-dollar bills.

"I never knew how Louis and Henry learned about the pack train and the cash it carried. But they did learn—with a gang, they held up the pack train, killed the two old prospectors, and got away with the money.

"They weren't very expert about it. They were suspected. They tried to drag Bruce and me into it. We weren't with Peele that night. I couldn't prove it, but I succeeded in making the sheriff believe in my innocence. The sheriff had come to our ranch after Bruce and me. After talking with me, he took his posse and went away. Bruce was not home. He hadn't come home the night before, from Tenville. He didn't come home that day. None of us ever saw Bruce again—alive."

"You saw him—dead?"

"I did, Doe. He disappeared. We could find no trace of him. Mother was frail; she was laid low by the shock. Harry Peele had disappeared, too. And Louis, who had done the killing. Louis *proved* that he hadn't been near the scene of the holdup. Things like that happen sometimes, Doe. The shock that had prostrated my mother killed her within three weeks. Two days after she was buried, a man came to the house at night, a big fat fellow called Porky Ellerton. I had seen him just once before, with Louis Peele, the day before the holdup.

"When I asked what he wanted of me, he said he knew where Bruce was, that if I would go with him, he would take me to Bruce and Harry. I asked just what was back of his coming to me that way, and he said he would tell me later. I went with him.

"It was a two-day ride we took. He led me to the slope behind Hell's Hill, so far back into the wilderness, so deep into timber and across canyons, that I wondered how he could find his way. But he knew what he was after, and he went straight to it—a pile of leaves and rocks in a thicket. He got off his horse and tore the leaves and rocks away. You can guess what was there."

"Bruce?" Doe's tongue was thick. "And—Harry Peele?"

"Right. Both of them had been shot to pieces. They had been dead for nearly four weeks. I took from Bruce's little finger the ring my father had given him. It is this ring, Doe." Hardin held up his right hand. On his little finger was a plain gold seal ring, engraved with the initials, *B H*. "I turned away, and told Ellerton to cover up the bodies. He did it, and followed me back to our horses. Then I learned what he hoped to gain by coming to me.

"He openly admitted that he wanted to rouse me

against Louis Peele. 'Louis did that!' he said, pointing to the heap where Bruce and Harry lay. 'He killed them both. I saw him do it. Killed Bruce, and his own brother Harry!'

"I asked what Bruce was doing there. 'Why, that holdup was pulled right back there,' he said. 'Bruce was coming back from Tenville, and he ran into us in the hills. He got curious as to what we were up to and followed us. After the holdup, Harry tried to stop one of the gang from getting away with the cash. Harry got it and started to run with it. Bruce jumped in and tried to take it from Harry. Louis shot them both down. And you—you have to get Louis Peele.'

" 'Why don't you get him yourself?' I said. He answered that he was afraid to try it. He was a poor shot. I've always been a good shot. He knew it. Well, I believed that Porky was telling the truth. But I didn't *know* it. That is, I couldn't prove it. Louis, remember, had *proved* that he wasn't near the scene of the holdup at the time it had taken place. I went back to the ranch a very sick boy, Doc. My entire family was gone. I was utterly alone. With the help of the sheriff I sold the ranch and got out of there.

"Before I left, three men of Peele's gang had been arrested, tried, convicted, and sent to the penitentiary. They were all men I had never seen before—a little rat with mean eyes, George Sidney; a gun-toting fellow named Jean Bluex; and a big ugly bruiser with a curly beard, Halvord Creegan, called 'Vord.' I saw them only at a distance, as the sheriff was taking them to jail. The week I left there, Porky Ellerton was found dead at the base of Hell's Hill. He had tried to get Louis after all, and had failed—but nobody could prove it."

"And you drifted down this way, and bought this ranch," Doc added thoughtfully. "And Louis found you out, and followed you. Why?"

Hardin sighed. "I think I know, Doc, boy. I have never

stopped trying to get something definite on Louis. He must realize that. Ever since he came here, I have held my hand and waited for him to break loose and give himself away.

"He knows how I loved Bruce. He's afraid I will find evidence against him some time, and he's bound to get rid of me, no matter what the price. He will never rest easy so long as I live. But he is too cunning to shoot me down in cold blood. He doesn't want to hang, nor go to the penitentiary for life as those three of his gang did. He wants to force me to fight, so that he can kill me—in self-defense."

"Oh!" breathed Doe again. "I'm beginning to see clear."

"Yes. He's on the rough edge, Doe. Yet—I know without asking you that there is no proof that he and his men killed Lonny Pope."

"You're right." Gaston lifted miserable eyes to Hardin's face. "There's no proof that he carried Mary Silver off, either. But we all reckon he did. He knew well enough that her brother Mel had gone in to Pendleton to ride in the roundup, and that she was therefore there alone. He got the hands of the J Bar B all riding along the Diamond W line, helping Warde's outfit—trying to catch some rustler that had been raiding the herds of both ranches. *He* was the rustler. But can we prove it? Hell, no! And while all the men of the Valley were down there, Mary disappeared. I know as well as you do who did it all, but none of us has any more proof than a jack rabbit."

"What did you do when you found Lon?" demanded Hardin.

"I went straight to the J Bar B taking Lon with me. I didn't dare accuse any one till I had something to go on. I did say that Louis Peele might have some knowledge of what had happened to Lon. The J Bar B crew don't love Louis any better than the Diamond W boys do, o'course. We all went flying down to Peele's ranch. It was plumb deserted, Gage. Not a soul there. Not a thing out of order, not a suspicious sign. That was when I went south after you.

"When I got back—what do you guess? One of Peele's men came in, as smooth as cream. He said he had come back to take care of the ranch till Louis and the rest of the crew returned; that they had gone to Pendleton to the round-up and he had ridden with them as far as Sky Gulch. Could anything sound more reasonable? And how were we to prove that he wasn't telling the truth?

"Even Warde and Baker cooled off. They told me I shouldn't go off half-cocked and get dangerous notions against Louis and his outfit till I had some proof to back me up, even if we didn't any of us like them too well. What was there left for me to do, Gage?"

"Exactly what you did do, Doe—send for Guy Shawnessy. It's a damn mess. The Four from Hell's Hill gone with the sheriff to hunt Louis Peele! But we can't waste time sitting here shooting the breeze, Doe. Mel will be getting back from the round-up——"

"But he won't!" Doe interrupted. "A bad horse piled him and broke his left hip. He'll have to stay there in the hospital for months. We just got word."

"That's bad, Doe! Bad for him, and for us, right now when we need him too——" Hardin cut himself short, as there came from the night outside the drumming sound of a horse's hoofs, approaching at a hard gallop. He turned his head swiftly to stare at Gaston.

They sat rigid, listening. The wildly running horse reached the lane, raced down it, and came to a staggering blowing halt in the rear yard near the house. The sound of a man's spur chains clinked through the silent night, as the rider of the horse heaved himself from the saddle and advanced toward the house.

Hardin sprang to his feet, half drawing his right-hand

gun. He leaped to the door and swung it open.

Guy Shawnessy lurched up the back steps and staggered across the porch. Hardin fell back a step as the sheriff stumbled into the room.

Shawnessy was hatless. His thick, blond, curling hair was matted with blood that had oozed from a wound in the scalp above his right temple. His pale face was streaked with blood and grime, drawn with pain and weariness.

His clothes were torn in numerous places and caked with dirt. His left arm hung limp. The shirt over his left shoulder was bullet-torn and dark with blood. There was a bullet hole in the top of his right boot, but the bullet which had made it had barely scored the skin.

In his arm he held Mary Silver. The right arm gripped her against his chest. Her lax body was further supported by the suspenders he had removed and tied about his body and hers for the purpose.

Her clothes were soiled and torn, also, spotted with blood from his wounds, but she was uninjured. Her face was drawn and white under the grime of dust and sweat. Racked by terror, vitiated by exhaustion, she was as soundly asleep as a person drugged.

Doe gaped at them, with appalled eyes, utterly unconscious of his scant garb.

Shawnessy turned a glassy gaze on Hardin. He seemed to be striving fully to convince himself that he had reached his destination at last. "Take her, Gage. Quick, man!"

Hardin dropped his half-drawn gun into its holster, slammed shut the door, and leaped to meet Shawnessy's swaying figure, all in one coordinated movement. He jerked asunder the suspenders that held Mary Silver's knees to the sheriff's side.

As he took her unconscious body into his arms, Shawnessy, relieved of the dead weight, closed his eyes and fell forward on his face.

CHAPTER VI

"GET your clothes on, Doe." Hardin turned to his trans-fixed partner.

Doe darted into his bedroom. Hardin carried Mary Silver into his own room and laid her gently on his bed. He covered her carefully and tiptoed from the room. He found Doe Gaston leaning over the sheriff, fully clothed.

Between them they lifted Shawnessy to the cot bed there in the main room and sought to ascertain the extent of his injuries. They knew enough about wounds to make a fair estimate of his state. Hardin drew himself erect with a breath of relief.

"He'll come out of it, Doe. The scalp wound isn't bad. The shoulder wound is clean, right through the flesh. The hole lower down in the arm is clean, too. Call Mitch Lord and send him for Jeff Baker. I'll get Guy straightened around."

Doe left the room without making any useless reply. Hardin fetched a basin of water and set to work to rid Shawnessy of blood and grime. He cut the blood-stiffened sleeve clear of the flesh, thinking that Baker would know what to do.

Baker had been a doctor before he had decided to cease giving pills and become a rancher. He himself would do what he could before Baker arrived. He got a clean flour sack and tore it up, in order to bandage the sheriff's wounds, and all the time Shawnessy lay like a dead man. But when Hardin began to wash the blood and dirt from the sheriff's face, Shawnessy gasped and looked up into the countenance above him with a drawn smile.

46

"I'm all right, Gage. I managed to collect a few holes and lose a little blood. That won't kill me."

Hardin returned the smile. "Right. You'll pull out of this in good order. Where are the Four from Hell's Hill, Guy?"

Shawnessy's face drew into harsh lines. "Dead, Gage. Louis Peele got them. Every man jack of them. Doe said you wanted to see Louis incriminate himself. He has done it. I saw him there, with his whole outfit. The Four tried to hold him off while I got Mary away. It was Louis Peele who shot me up, trying to down me before I could escape his fire. Gage, the last thing I saw there was the whole lot of them closing in on the Four, and—is that enough? They have shot an officer of the law—and the officer saw them clearly enough to identify them. Is that enough for you?"

"Plenty!"

Shawnessy gasped, and sank back into unconsciousness, just as Doe Gaston rushed into the room to report that Mitch Lord had gone to bring Jeff Baker.

"Louis got the Four," Hardin said, as Doe halted beside the bed on which the sheriff lay. "Every one of them. Guy saw it; he saw Louis' crew close in on the Four. I have Louis Peele at last, Doe. It was Louis himself who shot Guy. Take this basin and finish cleaning the sheriff up, Doe. I'm going in to see that Mary is all right."

He handed the basin to Gaston, and went swiftly into his room, where Mary Silver lay.

He lighted a lamp which filled the room with subdued light. She lay exactly as Hardin had left her, on his homely bed, his blanket thrown lightly over her, still in the sleep of utter exhaustion.

Hardin paused at the head of the bed, looking down at her, really scarcely seeing her, striving to envision the terror and indignity she must have experienced at the hands of Louis Peele. Then he dropped to his knees by the bed, suddenly realizing how much he was vitiated and shaken; his head leaned against her limp right hand.

An hour and a half later, when Mitch Lord rode galloping into the back yard in company with Jeff Baker, Guy Shawnessy had again regained consciousness. As Baker bent over the wounded man, to examine him with the deft touch that no few years of ranching could take from him, Doe Gaston stepped to the connecting door to call Hardin.

He opened his mouth to speak, but his tongue went still at what he saw. He backed away from the door on tiptoe.

Baker looked up inquiringly as Gaston approached him. Doe Gaston's smile was apologetic.

"He's gone fast asleep, sitting there on the floor by her, Jeff. How's Guy going to come along?"

Baker answered with the professional briskness of a doctor, with the air that would always return to him when he stepped into a sickroom. "He'll be pretty weak for several days. He's lost a lot of blood. But he'll do. Oh, yes, he'll do. However, it will be several weeks before he'll really be up again."

"Several weeks!" Shawnessy spoke from the bed. "You gents know I'm a peace officer. I have to get out of this and go after Peele, and I can't wait any several weeks to do it."

"I fear you'll have to," Baker answered, his attention instantly focused on the injured man. "You will not have anything to say about it, sheriff. I said several weeks. You'll have to abide by that. Your left arm is likely to be stiff for a while. Now, don't argue with me. You're here to stay. You're not going after Peele or anyone else. Doe and Gage will have to keep a watch on you. Your life really depends on it." He shot a grim glance at Gaston. "Remember that, Doe."

"Sure thing." Gaston looked down at Shawnessy with anxious eyes. "Some of the rest of us will go after Louis

Peele, Guy. I—well, maybe I had better keep my mouth shut. I have said too much already. But I didn't know then, when I sent for you, what was back of it. I am only saying now that all Gage needed was really to get something solid on Louis Peele. We seem to have it at last."

"We have."

Doe and Baker both whirled at the sound of the voice which had come from behind them. They saw Hardin bulking tall and dour in the doorway leading from the room in which Mary Silver lay asleep.

"I heard what you said just now, Jeff. I heard you, too, Doe. I can guess the rest. Yes, I have all I need on Louis Peele—at last."

Jeff Baker raised his brows in inquiry. "I fear that most of this is going over my head, Gage. But it's none of my business—why you should want to get anything on Louis Peele, or how you've gotten it. But I would say that, obviously, you have gotten plenty."

"Yes, plenty." Gage Hardin looked steadily down upon Shawnessy, but his eyes were seeing far beyond the sheriff's drawn face. "It was all hidden there, behind Hell's Hill. I always knew that some time, somehow, I'd get to the bottom of it. And the getting has begun."

CHAPTER VII

MORNING

THE clock struck eight as Mary Silver wakened the next morning, the small wooden clock with the coil gong that Gage Hardin kept on the shelf at the head of his bed. But Mary Silver had never seen the clock before. She had never seen the room before.

She listened for a moment, hearing voices outside the house within which she lay, and three lower voices conversing in the next room. She strove to catch an intelligible word from either source, even a tone that would ring familiar, but she heard nothing more than the rumble of indeterminate speech.

She sat up in the bed, finding herself very weak, and looked about herself curiously. She saw neither familiar clothes nor objects. She had no idea where she was.

She tried to remember what had happened. The last thing she could recall was seeing a dark figure crawling into the brush lean-to where Louis Peele and his men had left her helplessly bound. Her first thought had been that the crawling figure was Louis Peele. She quivered, remembering her start of terror, then her wild surge of relief at the sound of a voice she had recognized as belonging to Guy Shawnessy.

She remembered that the sheriff had set her free, had told her to follow him. She remembered that she had crawled after him, that he had lifted her in his arms and started to run. She remembered nothing more, beyond the sudden blast of gunfire, Red Corcoran's voice cursing furiously, and other voices retorting in savage defiance. Nothing more.

Her first thought was that the attempt at rescue had failed, that Peele's men had taken her from Shawnessy. She glanced down at her clothes, and she saw that they were splotched with dried blood. She knew whose blood it was. "Guy!" She repressed a shiver of sheer terror. "They got him. But where have they taken me?"

She mustered all the strength remaining to her, slipped from the bed to the floor, determined to learn where she was. For a moment she stood swaying in weakness, gripping the head of the bed for support.

Then she gained her balance and made her way to the closed door a few feet beyond. She leaned against the door, striving to catch some word from those three men conversing in the adjoining room, some word that might enlighten her. She heard, very clearly:

"You'll have to do as Jeff says, Guy. You're pretty badly shot up. You go after Peele in your present condition and you'll be carrion before morning. You leave Louis Peele to me. You've done your share, bringing Mary back safe." The voice was that of Gage Hardin.

Mary swung open the door with a cry that was blended of hysteria and relief, to see Guy Shawnessy lying in the cot bed in the next room, to see Doe Gaston sitting on a chair at the foot of the bed, and Hardin himself standing at the head of it looking down at the wounded sheriff.

Her cry swept through the room like the wail of a high wind. Gaston leaped to his feet. Shawnessy turned his head. Hardin whirled, and leaped toward her as she swayed on her feet. He moved barely in time to save her from falling. Limp, she wilted against him.

He lifted her and carried her to a chair beside a table against the wall, where she could sit facing all three of them.

She gave him a wan smile, still too shaken by sheer relief to regain her voice wholly. "I—I didn't know where I was, Gage. I thought Louis—I thought he still———"

Hardin reached out a hand to grip hers in instant reassurance.

"Easy, now. Pull yourself together, Mary. Everything's all right. Guy isn't hurt seriously. He simply has to be quiet. Let us think about you. Is there anything we can do for you? Could you possibly eat something?"

Doc Gaston was already on his feet, moving toward the small lean-to kitchen adjoining the room at the farther end.

"What will I get, Gage?"

Hardin frowned. "Not too much, Doc. A soft-boiled egg. Toast, butter, coffee." He smiled at Mary Silver. "And don't make the coffee strong enough to float a horseshoe, Doc. And don't break the egg yolk, nor burn the toast. But you *could* hurry."

The kitchen door swung shut upon Doc's hearty answer:

"Hurry? You know it! Hang on, Mary. I'll have your breakfast in a jiffy."

Hardin's gaze swung back to Mary Silver. "When you get some food inside your stomach, do you think you will feel up to telling us what happened, Mary?"

"You see, Mary," Shawnessy put in gently, "we have to *know*. We have to be *sure* just how far Louis Peele is answerable to the law. Guessing won't do."

For the first time since she had entered the room, Mary Silver turned her gaze upon Guy Shawnessy's pale face. She thought of the blood on her own clothes. Wounds received, for her. Blood shed, for her. Life offered, for her. No woman is proof against that. Her gaze grew tender, brooding.

"I understand, Guy. Certainly guessing won't do. Of course you have to know. But there's no necessity for waiting. I can tell you now." Her gaze swerved to Hardin, and for a moment she thought she saw a sudden pain, a swift fear written upon his face.

She did not err. The pain and fear were there. He had

never seen her look at Shawnessy that way before. She read the look in Hardin's face, but she was too wise to let him see that she had read it. Her gaze went back to Shawnessy.

Mary frowned. "The whole thing's rather queer, Guy. Red Corcoran came to my cabin, saying that Doe had sent him, to be sure that I was all right. He said Doe was tied up at the ranch because of some trouble about the horses."

"That's correct," Gaston called from the kitchen.

"Well, that much is straight." Mary glanced at Hardin, with concealed uneasiness. "I was just starting out for a ride. Red didn't want me to go alone. He just insisted that, if I was going for a ride, he would accompany me. What could I say? He had alarmed me, and I made no objection to being guarded.

"We rode for a short distance, then I decided I had better stay at home. I told Red so, and started back myself. He made me promise to go straight home. Well—I didn't do it. I rode over the hill to the little spring at the foot of Bald Peak to get a drink and to water my horse; it wasn't much out of my way.

"Two of Peele's men jumped me there by the spring, and they weren't any too gentle about it either. I screamed. I thought maybe Red might hear me. One of Peele's men slapped me across the mouth and threatened to knock me unconscious if I made another sound. I was afraid to——"

Hardin interrupted with an unintelligible exclamation. Shawnessy's mouth set, but he said nothing. Mary swallowed a gasp, and her face whitened at the memory.

"Gage! I was frightened out of my wits. They blindfolded me, gagged me, tied me onto my horse, and after that I was so downright terrified that I didn't know much what was happening. We continued riding, we camped at night. They kept me tied all the time. They would give me nothing to eat. I could smell the food they were cooking at the campfire. I was so hungry——"

Hardin lurched from his chair, his control almost broken. Just then the kitchen door swung open, and Doe Gaston came striding into the room, a smoking plate in one hand and a cup of steaming coffee in the other. On the plate reposed a poached egg perfectly cooked and two slices of toast.

"This is where you eat, Mary," Doe announced briskly. "I think we know all we want to know, without you saying any more, don't we, Gage?"

"I knew enough, years ago." Hardin carefully moved Mary's chair close to the table as Doe Gaston placed the food before her. "Only—I had no proof. But now, you, Mary—you *saw* Louis Peele—Guy saw him——"

The girl raised her eyes as she reached eager fingers for a slice of toast.

"No, Gage. I didn't *see* Louis. I wish I could say that I had seen him, but I can't. I had never seen before the two men who took me. I'm certain they were Peele's men, but I can't prove it. I didn't *see* them with Louis Peele. I didn't once *see* Louis Peele himself. I heard a voice several times, a voice I could swear was his. But that wouldn't go very far in a court of law, Gage. Guy knows that."

"What of it?" Shawnessy smiled from his pillow. "I saw him and his men close in on the Four from Hell's Hill. I took his lead in my shoulder. Peele was the man who had you then, so it must have been Peele's men who took you, and that's not circumstantial evidence. That's plain cold mathematics."

CHAPTER VIII

LEAVE-TAKING

MARY moved her chair back from the table. Her gaze, brooding, rested upon Gage Hardin, sitting directly across the room from her, cleaning and oiling his guns.

"Gage, you are not going out after Louis Peele and his gang right away, are you?"

Hardin raised one brief glance to meet her eyes. "Soon as I can, Mary."

The girl smothered a sigh of resignation. "I suppose it's the only way. Someone has to get sign of them before they are too far gone into the mountains. I could wish that Great Lost Valley wasn't so isolated."

"Yes," Hardin agreed. "I purposely looked for a place in the wilds, certain never to be too popular with folks. Rugged enough in its character and surroundings to keep most people from settling. I seem to have found it." He raised one gun and squinted through the barrel.

"Very convenient—for Louis Peele," said Shawnessy from the bed. "He's headed straight back into the wilderness where there's no more than a scattered, struggling ranch here and there, a prospector or two, and all of them so far apart that they are of no practical value in a case like this. Just the same, I can sure enough direct you to the exact place in which I found Peele and his men. That's a start, anyhow."

He went on talking rapidly, in brief but comprehensive words giving Hardin the location of the camp where Peele had been halted when he had overtaken him.

"They were not difficult to trail, of course. They were expecting *you* to follow them, and they left you aplenty of

55

easy sign. They were startled out of a year's growth when it was I who came on them, with the Four. That's the only reason I ever got away alive. Their surprise threw them just enough off guard that the Four had time to engage their attention till I was free of pursuit. I suppose they wouldn't have pursued me, anyway. All they want is to draw you after them. Well, they've succeeded in forcing that. You keep your eyes open, Gage."

"Reckon I'd better." Hardin rose to his feet, twirling the cylinders of the guns in turn, giving them a last-minute scrutiny. Then he shoved them into their holsters.

"I'm going with you," announced Doe Gaston. "My old Winchester ain't rusty."

Hardin turned a cool gaze on him. "You are doing nothing of the kind. You are needed worse on the Circle Crossbar than you are anywhere else. You are staying here with Mary and the boys, and taking care of the ranch. The five of you will have aplenty to keep you busy. Right now, you can go saddle Chaser for me, if you will."

Doe rose and quitted the room without protest. Hardin turned to the sheriff.

"Guy, what there is about this feud that you don't know, Doe does know. He can make full explanation to you after I'm gone. I'll tell him to. Hope you're on your feet soon."

Shawnessy's eyes were on the woman they both loved as she followed Hardin out to the porch. The door closed. Outside, Mary Silver drew close to Gage Hardin, lifting her gaze to his. He bent toward her.

"Mary, with Guy lying wounded, somebody else has to go after Louis Peele. Because of what happened once, the job is mine. After you have talked with Doe, you will understand why Louis and me are overdue for a showdown. You know how much I love you, Mary."

"I do. But—no more than I love you, Gage. And that love goes with you. It might even—protect you."

His arms went around her and held her close. "It will, Mary. Don't worry about me. I'll take good care. But remember all we've planned. I know the wild territory into which I'm going. I know Louis Peele. I may be gone for a long time. But if we can both believe it hard enough— I'll come back."

She had no articulate answer. He kissed her, thrust her from him, went down the steps and across the yard, stumbling a little, as though his sight was blurred.

Mary Silver leaned against the closed door, stifling a sob in her throat. She did not move again until she saw Hardin reach the barn, saw Doe lead out the gray gelding, saw Hardin lift himself to the saddle and ride away between the trees that lined the lane leading to the road.

Doe lowered his head and came plodding toward the house. Mary opened the door, walked unseeing into the room, and crossed the floor to sink on her knees beside Shawnessy's bed. She made no sound. Shawnessy's hand lifted and settled to rest on her bowed head.

Doe Gaston stopped at the open door. His gaze met Shawnessy's and held. Doe was not in the habit of putting his thoughts into words. Which fact did not hinder the clarity of his thoughts. As he stood there holding Shawnessy's gaze, something communicated itself between the two men, a warning, a hope, a fear.

That girl was the sum of all living to Gage Hardin, Doe thought, and Gage had been forced to leave her in the company of a man who loved her fully as well as he—a man who had brought her safe out of dire danger, who had offered his life and lost his blood to accomplish the bringing. And while Gage was absent, she would be nursing Shawnessy back to strength, having constantly held before her the worth of the man proved by what he had done.

Shawnessy read his thoughts on his face. "There goes a man, Doe."

"Yes." Doe nodded, and advanced slowly into the room. "And he's gone on a hard journey. But—sometimes—what lies ahead of a man, Guy, is easier to take than the danger he has left behind him."

Shawnessy smiled. "The minute I can travel, I'm going after him, Doe. We both know—I must get out of here."

CHAPTER IX

ELK CROSSING

CASPER LOODY, who kept a small trail store at Elk Crossing, deep in the mountains, miles from any town, was putting shelves to rights before locking up for the night. He was a very methodical man. He never left his store in disorder.

The night was very dark. The thin crescent moon gave little light. Loody shoved a box back on a shelf, yawned behind his gray mustache, and turned—to face a man who had silently entered the store while Loody's back was turned. Loody gasped and stood still.

The man bulked big and dark, dusty with the signs of long travel. His face was half hidden by the hat pulled low over black eyes. A short black beard and mustache covered the lower part of his face. The beard was squared, notably spadeshaped. Two guns were slung conspicuously about his waist on crossed belts. Neither was drawn.

The intruder gave Loody a deprecating smile. "I suppose I look scarey, hey? Sorry. Please don't make any fuss. I'm not holding you up."

Loody scowled and relaxed a little from his instant of fright. "What do you want?"

The big man's smile grew humorous. "Well, I want food, that's all—and I want to keep out of sight. That's why I waited till you were alone. I must have food, and I happen to have run out of money. If you'll get me a few cans of beans, a loaf of bread, and a little bacon, I'll be obliged to you, mister."

Loody stared at him with open resentment. "I don't allow credit. I can't afford to feed all the tinhorn tramps that come——"

59

"I'm no tramp," the big man interrupted. His voice sharpened with impatience. "I've told you I have no money. But I will have it later, and I'll see that you get it."

Loody shrugged and turned to his shelves. He took down a loaf of bread, four cans of beans, a generous slab of bacon, and slammed the articles on the counter. He favored the big man with a boring gaze, as the other picked up the foodstuffs.

The big man smiled again. "Keep this little business to yourself, will you? My name is Hardin. Gage Hardin. I'm a stranger in your territory. I'm here after a gent who's made his escape up this way—the kind of snake you'd shoot at sight, if you knew what he'd done. I'll send you the money for this stuff at my first chance. What do I owe you?"

"Not a cent, if you're telling the truth," Loody answered. "If you aren't—I wouldn't want to be in your boots."

Hardin laughed. "Well, that will prove itself. Thank you again." He turned and walked out of the store.

Loody stood listening till he heard the sound of a horse departing at a swift gait. Then he advanced down his counter, rounded the end of it, and went on to the open door. The man was riding straight down the trail, headed northeast.

"Hm-m-m!" Loody muttered to himself. "It sounds fishy. I'll remember that fellow. He must have been about six feet four. Black hair, black eyes, black spade beard. I wonder if that was his real name? Gage Hardin. I'll certainly keep you in mind, Mr. Hardin!"

A mile down the road Hardin turned into the timber that blanketed the mountains through which for long, profitless days he had followed the trail of Louis Peele.

From the tracks he had found and had been able to segregate, he estimated that there must be a dozen men in all, including Louis Peele. Louis had had five men on his ranch, excluding the one remaining behind as a blind. He must have added six or seven men to his group. He might have had them in the background somewhere, aiding him in his raids.

Too weary to indulge in lengthy speculating, Hardin rode on, with the aid of his gray horse choosing his way between the trees into a deep canyon and on to a spot beside a mountain creek. There he halted, unsaddled Chaser in the dark, and found a place between rearing boulders where he could build a small fire without danger of detection from some lone passer-by. He ate, turned his horse to graze, fixed a bough bed for the night, and put out the fire.

He lay awake for a while, harassed by thoughts that would not be banished easily. Mind pictures kept pace with the thoughts—the appearance of the camp where Shawnessy had taken Mary Silver from Peele and his men; the rock cairn, crude but decidedly efficient and cunningly hidden in a canyon, where he had removed only rocks enough to ascertain that under them lay the bodies of four men, and had replaced the rock hastily at the sight of Red Corcoran's green-checked flannel shirt.

The Four from Hell's Hill. And somewhere behind that hill lay all that he wanted to know. Hardin frowned in the dark, remembering. He felt certain that Peele and his small outfit had committed that robbery and killing at Hell's Hill so long ago. He felt quite as certain that Ellerton had told him the truth.

Had he not himself seen the bodies of Harry Peele and Bruce lying there behind the hill in the leaves, under the rocks? And Hardin knew within himself that Peele had killed Ellerton and left him there on the slope of Hell's Hill. Just as he had killed Lonny Pope and left him in the doorway of Mary Silver's cabin for Doe Gaston to find. The score against Louis Peele was high.

He yawned, with a last thought for logic. *Was* it logic that Peele could have gone to such lengths merely because of fear of what he, Hardin, might know? Or was there some more vital thing that drove Peele, something that Hardin had not guessed? That was the last thought in Hardin's brain as he fell asleep there in the canyon.

CHAPTER X

THE PUZZLE

ON the Circle Crossbar, Hardin was right then a subject of conversation. Shawnessy, who was now sitting up and getting around a little, was a subject, also, and a subject of concern, to Doe Gaston and Mary Silver. Still more a subject of concern perhaps to Jeff Baker, who felt his responsibility in the matter.

As Baker had predicted, Shawnessy's left arm was proving stiff and unmanageable. His slowly healing wounds were painful and troublesome. The sheriff was harassed by his inability to follow Hardin, his fear being that the chase might be over before he was well enough to take the trail.

The three in the ranch house on the Circle Crossbar were all prey to fear. Mary Silver feared that Gage Hardin might never come back. Doe Gaston feared that if he did come back, he might wish he hadn't.

He watched Mary and Shawnessy, and at the look he surprised a few times on their faces he was almost guilty of wishing that Hardin *wouldn't* return. He came in from the corral, having cared for his horse after the day's work, to find Mary and the sheriff talking.

"It simply is not reasonable," Shawnessy was saying as Doe entered the room. "Admit that, Mary. You can't avoid it. I've not been able to get it off my mind since Doe told me what happened in the Hell's Hill territory."

"What isn't reasonable?" Doe asked, halting just inside the outer door. "What's on your mind, Guy?"

Shawnessy moved his wounded shoulder to a more comfortable position against his pillows. "Why, the idea that Peele would have followed Gage here after years went by,

Doe. You know it isn't reasonable. Even a man like Peele must have some hell of a strong reason for such a course of action. How much money was taken from that pack train, Doe? Did Gage ever say?"

"Yes." Doe advanced into the room and seated himself in a chair facing the sheriff. "Seventy-five thousand dollars, all in one-thousand-dollar bills."

He paused, thinking over what Shawnessy had said concerning Peele's motives.

"Not reasonable? No, of course it isn't. I've been thinking that the money must have something to do with it. Funny how loco men will go over a little money, but there's no argument there. They do it, that's all. Money could make a man like Louis Peele raise hell for a lifetime, if he thought he could lay hands on it and somebody else was keeping it from him. Isn't it possible, Guy, that Louis didn't get that seventy-five thousand dollars after all?"

"Of course it's possible. And seventy-five thousand is a lot of money, Doe."

"Louis might *believe* that Gage had gotten it, mightn't he?" Mary put in.

Shawnessy hesitated, frowning, then shook his head. "I don't see how he could think that, Mary. He knew that Gage had not been near the scene of the holdup, that he'd had nothing to do with it in any way."

"But you want to remember that Bruce was there," Doe reminded him.

"I'm not forgetting it, Doe. Neither am I forgetting that Bruce was killed before he could have even got hold of the money, and was buried there with Harry Peele. Yet the fact remains that Peele himself might have been telling the truth when he swore to Ellerton that he did not have the seventy-five thousand, that he did not know where it was. That was what Gage told you, wasn't it?"

"Yes." Gaston nodded. "We talked about it a little, just

before Gage lit out after Louis. Of course, Ellerton didn't believe Louis, that was why he wanted Gage to get rid of him, or get hold of him and make him come out with the truth, one of the two."

"Well, where's Louis' argument then?" Shawnessy demanded. "He knows Bruce couldn't have got the money and passed it to Gage, because he himself shot Bruce down right there before the money had disappeared. If Louis didn't get it, what became of it? With Bruce and Harry killed on the spot, with George Sidney, Jean Bluex, and Vord Creegan sent to prison for life, who could have gotten it? Yet I think you're right. I can find no possible solution to the question, but I'm convinced that the money is back of Peele's feuding with Gage. It's the only reasonable answer."

"Well, there has to be some answer, that's certain." Doe laughed, the kind of laugh that brings chill to a hearer's skin. "And if we think about it hard enough and long enough, we're likely to find it. What if we can't figure who got the money? That's no sign that Louis did get it. If we can find the answer to the puzzle by the time you're well enough to follow Gage, you'll have another weapon in your hand beside your gun, Guy."

"I'll need it," Shawnessy admitted grimly. "And I'm not going to stop working at the puzzle till I discover some plausible theory. Louis Peele has at least *thought* he had some good reason to follow Gage Hardin here, after all those years—and he must have *thought* Gage was hiding from him, and maybe believed Gage knew a lot more about that disappearing money than he's ever told. That, at least, would be a good reason for all the deviling of Gage that he has done. That money is just about the one thing that could drive a man like Peele to the lengths to which he has gone. He certainly acts as if he hadn't got it himself, after he held up the pack train. But if he didn't, who did? And why does he act so sure that Gage knows something about it?"

Doe Gaston rose from his chair. "Ask somebody to answer that who has more brains than I've got, Guy," he said, with a shrug. "If Gage were only here to go into more detail, he might shed some light on this pow-wow. As I told you, when he told me about it he was in a hurry, and I guess I got just the sketchiest possible story. But—he's not here."

He glanced covertly at Mary Silver, and in that glance was meaning, if the girl had recognized it for what it held.

"And I'd give a good deal to know just where he is about now, and what he's found," said Shawnessy. "He must be fifty miles from here now, and should have come up with Louis Peele and his mob a long time ago, if things had gone the way Peele intended them to go. All he wanted at first was to get a chance to ambush Gage. But since he knows I saw him, when I took you away, Mary, he's more interested in running from Gage as well as from everybody else. He knows what would happen to him if a posse should catch up with him." He frowned heavily. "What will happen to him if I ever do get well enough to head out after him with a posse." For a long minute he was thoughtful. "If he still thinks Gage knows anything about that money, it's my guess he won't give up trying to get Gage into his hands, no matter if he is on the run himself now."

The sheriff was conservative in his estimate of how far Gage Hardin had gone. At that very moment he was nearly a hundred miles away and going on, still grimly determined.

He was following a canyon that bore in its bed faint traces to indicate that Louis Peele and his men had passed that way. But then he had followed many such as he had gone doggedly on his pursuit.

In fact, it was to become legend in Great Lost Valley,

in the years to come, how Gage Hardin worked out that trail that Peele thought he had so cleverly hidden. A blind, twisted trail that was born in the clever twisted brain of Louis Peele to keep a posse from learning the whereabouts of his hideout while he lay there with his men, waiting for the proper chance to make another, and final attack on Gage Hardin.

In the days Hardin had been following he had found evidence that they had gone in this particular direction, however, for with his purpose in mind, his trailing scent was as keen as an Indian's. He had found their dead fires, even though they had been buried and apparently all sign of them destroyed. And it was near these fires that he had discovered that he was right in his theory that the horses' feet were covered with sacks, for he found traces of burlap bags which had been burned when new sacks had been put on the horses. Camp after camp he managed to locate, though they were spots so clean that ninety-nine men out of a hundred, seasoned trackers, would have sworn no camp had been made there at all, a fire ever built.

He followed sign across rangeland, through forests, and on into the foothills. Back onto the lower land, across high mesas, over hogbacks, through canyons so thick with timbered growth that it was all he could do to push his mount through. But he knew he was on the right track, for even in such spots, or in the more open places where clean rocks would show no traces of horses' hoofs, he was able to tell which way the men he wanted had gone by a displaced small stone here and there, or perhaps a bit of crushed moss.

Though the trail he was now following was, apparently, only a few hours old, there was no elation in Gage Hardin's heart when finally he had to give it up for a few hours when darkness fell. His horse was too spent to go further—and he was in need of rest himself. So long he had been in the saddle that he was half reeling with fatigue when he climbed to the ground and uncinched his saddle.

Hardin made a dry camp, hidden in a thick clump of woods, sheltering his horse in a small blind canyon. He was heartsick at the realization that Louis and his men had gained on him during the day, and he meant to rest only the fewest possible hours it would take his horse to recoup its strength.

But, as he had to acknowledge, it looked to him as though this were familiar ground to Peele—probably the hideout to which all the cattle rustled in the Valley had been brought, for a long time—and it was all strange terrain to him. Gritting his teeth, he determined that this should make no difference eventually, however, and with a sigh ate some of his cold rations and lay down with his saddle for a pillow for his much-needed rest.

Even then, he could not sleep at once, though, for the whole problem haunted him. He could not figure it out. Lying on the ground, with his face turned to the stars, he fretted again at Louis Peele's actions until his brain was once more weary with the same old round and round of thought.

Why had Peele followed him to Great Lost Valley, when all he, Gage Hardin, had wanted to do was get out of the man's sight, to try to forget him forever, since it was impossible for him to prove that Louis Peele had killed his brother Bruce. And then there had been that promise—the promise he had given his heartbroken mother. She had known so little of men, of bad men, in spite of being a pioneer woman herself.

She had known Louis and Harry Peele since they had been little fellows, playing with her own sons. She had not been able to force herself, even when everything looked so black against him, to believe Louis had killed Bruce and his own brother Harry. And she had begged for that promise from Gage—that he would never exact payment of a blood debt from Louis Peele until he could *prove* that the man was guilty.

Well, he could exact enough from Louis now. Perhaps he still could not prove that Louis had himself murdered Bruce and Harry—but there was something else now. Louis *was* a killer—he had committed the overt act, as Doc Gaston had said. Lonny Pope was dead—and his death lay straight at the door of Peele and his men.

And Guy Shawnessy was proof that it had been Louis who had carried Mary Silver off.

That was enough. Looking harder at the stars, Gage Hardin was convinced that now his mother would know he was taking the right course—and she would approve.

But first, of course, he had to find Louis. And if only he could get an answer to Louis' actions now, after all these nine years! He finally had reached the point now where he had to concede to himself that it probably was the money from the pack train that Peele had held up that was responsible.

In some ways it was beginning to look as if Porky Ellerton had told the truth when he had said that Peele had not got the money after all. And he would never give up until he did track it down, find out who had got it, and wrest it from that man.

But what did the money from that pack train robbery have to do with him, with Gage Hardin? He certainly did not have the money in his possession, nor did he know the first thing about it. Surely Peele should have known after nine years, when Hardin had shown no indication of any prosperity he did not earn with his own hands, that the money was elsewhere.

What was more, as Peele should long ago have reasoned out, he, Hardin, had no way whatsoever of knowing what could have become of the proceeds of that robbery. Certainly he had been nowhere near the pack train when it was held up and the men killed—as well as his brother Bruce and Harry Peele.

Lying there under night's dark canopy, until drowsiness, then sleep, finally claimed him, Hardin reached no answer to all the questions that were running riot in his mind; no answer to his puzzles. Perhaps it may have been just as well, at that time, that he did not, for the true answer to that problem of Louis Peele's vengeful quest was so bitterly harsh and incredible that Gage Hardin could not have chanced upon it in his wildest imaginings. Could he have known just what was back of the entire tangle that so bewildered him, he would have cried out in rank unbelief that life could play such a grim trick on a man as was in the process of being played on him.

But he did not know. And half of life is tragic or ghastly, half of the world's bitterness and sorrow comes to pass simply because of the regrettable fact that somebody "didn't know."

CHAPTER XI

IN PEELE'S CAMP

SEVERAL miles in advance of Gage Hardin, cleverly concealed in a deep gully and adequately guarded by verdure terrain against observation or surprise attack, the Peele outfit had also stopped for the night.

Louis Peele was sitting beside a dying campfire, in company with ten other men, most of them men who had been with him for years in his long life of pillage. Others were newcomers, but had been brought under Peele's sway as he had collected all his men—through intimidation because of something the keen-witted Peele had learned of them that would earn them a hangman's rope should he turn them in to the law.

In looks, Peele himself was as different from the men he had gathered about him as it was possible for human masculinity to be. In another environment he would have been called "dapper," even after the hardships of long days' riding.

He was a handsome, tigerish sort of man, but there was the dangerous glitter of steel in his eyes which, when he smiled, never changed their expression. He smiled only—when he did smile—with the muscular movement of his lips.

"This thing is starting to get on my nerves," he asserted, his impatience with the world and things in general plainly evident in face and voice. "You four"—he indicated in a sweeping gesture four men across the fire from him—"have been with me for nearly six years. You never saw me give up a thing once I had started it—and I don't mean to now, even if some things were bungled and set the law on our trail.

71

"You three there—you, Boole, Soapy and Hatteras, I mean—you are beginning to learn it, if you haven't been with this outfit for so long. And you other three—" the hand swept out to indicate the grouchy-looking three men who had not before been included—"had better take it into consideration." He scowled at the last three men of the group, who were seated on logs at his left.

Those three men, Dutch Sundquist, Tamm Oaks, and Salt River Charley, had been just a few days with this outlaw organization, and it was with no voluntary pleasure that they were here now. The three men left of the Four from Hell's Hill were forcibly in rôles new to them.

"So what?" Oaks growled.

Louis Peele glared at him with his cold, smileless eyes.

"So this," he said. "I don't care to hear any more grumbling such as I heard out of you last night, Oaks. That's all. Unless you want to get what Red Corcoran got. Haven't I warned you enough? Don't you know I'm going through with this thing, and that not you, nor any man on earth can stop me?"

Oaks repressed a shiver he never could help when those cold eyes looked into his. For a moment an ugly fire burned in his own eyes, but he quickly lowered his gaze so that Peele could not see it.

Dutch Sundquist sat motionless, his gaze on the fire, and said nothing. But as it seemed that some sort of comment was called for, Salt River Charley took it upon himself to answer the leader of the band.

"We agreed only to make no attempt to escape," he said flatly. "And to give you a chance to prove your claims about Hardin."

"You agreed!" Peele laughed. "I like your way of putting it! You agreed—yes, after you were knocked down and disarmed, and held to watch what we did to Red. That was a lesson for you three, you know. I have use for you. And

I was telling you straight facts. You manage to remain patient a little longer and you'll get the shock of your lives, if you are still believing in Gage Hardin.

"How he fooled all of you back in the Valley for so long is more than I can figure out. But then, he's smooth. I've known him long enough to realize just how smooth he is. He has simply been lying low till he considered it safe to spend that cash he took from the pack train. I told you that I knew if I could only worry him enough to get him started, he would show himself for what he was. You wait a little longer, and you'll see the proof of what I told you."

"Oh, yes?" Dutch Sundquist raised his gaze from the fire to Peele's face. "Well, what can we do but wait? We —didn't exactly want what Red got, as you so neatly put it. So—we're still here and kicking. Why do you keep on yowling at us, Peele? We have no weapons, you keep us guarded and hemmed in day and night. Why all the suspicion? We're playing your game, aren't we?"

Peele grunted a sour monosyllable.

"Why not let us all be as friendly as we can?" Sundquist persisted. "You have set me thinking, Louis. As you wanted to do. You've talked for days about that holdup which took place so long ago. How can you be so sure that Hardin got that money?"

"I've told you," Peele answered impatiently. "It disappeared from the spot after the fight was over. Harry tried to get it. It wasn't much to handle, you know. Just a small iron box containing seventy-five one-thousand-dollar bills. Harry was crooked; I didn't dare let him get his hands on it. I had to stop him. Bruce tried to take it from him. I had to down the two of them to keep from losing the cash —and then did lose it after all. Bruce had no business interfering. He only got what was coming to him."

"And you told that fellow Ellerton to cart Bruce and Harry off and bury 'em," Tamm Oaks mused. "Was that it?"

"Ellerton *and* Vord Creegan," Peele corrected. "They did as I told them to do, lugged off the bodies of Harry and Bruce, while Jean and George buried the two fellows who had had the pack train. But where they slipped, Porky and Creegan, was in not coming right on back after burying Bruce and Harry. They kept going. The posse trailed Creegan. Porky got away. He told me that after they had buried the bodies, he went one way and Creegan another.

"Porky was never under suspicion. I proved myself in the clear. Creegan, Jean, and George got the works. I stayed in the hills for a while, wanting to be sure I was clear. Porky got the crazy idea that I had the money, he hunted me out and tried to make me divide what I didn't have. I was forced to kill him to save my own life. Naturally I got out of there then."

"Queer you'd go away and leave all that cash lying around for somebody else to find," Tamm Oaks commented.

"Nobody ever found it," Peele retorted. "And how could I know where it had gone? I went to the jail to see Creegan. That didn't buy me anything. Then I came back to have it out with Gage, but he'd sold his ranch and gone. Nobody knew *where* he'd gone, either. I thought then, and I think still, that he was hidden right there at the holdup watching the whole show, that he got the money and hid it somewhere.

"I roamed around alone for a couple of years till the affair was about forgotten, then I began picking up fighting men. We would have a stronger force if Shawnessy hadn't succeeded in getting three we buried back there with Corcoran. But he slipped up on us. I wasn't looking for the sheriff and a posse to trail us. I was looking for Hardin alone."

"It was you who slipped, Louis," said Salt River Charley.

"I didn't slip!" snapped Peele. "I simply didn't think Doe Gaston would have the foolhardiness to call the sheriff into it. I simply figured on hitting hard enough to draw Gage into action. Doe played my hand when he called

Gage back from chasing Rood Vandover; I figured he'd do that. But he pulled a fast one when he sent for Shawnessy without even waiting for Gage to get back. He got panicky.

"There was no reason for it. We wouldn't have hurt the girl. Why argue about what's done and can't be undone? It's what lies ahead of us that we have to think about. You fellows keep your eyes open. Hardin isn't going to be much longer about breaking loose."

"So you tracked him down, and badgered him for four years, just because you believe he got that money?" Salt River Charley inquired.

"Isn't that enough?" Peele demanded. "It was my money. I held the pack train up for it, didn't I? In all the years I trailed Gage Hardin, I found certain proof that he never spent that money any place. He still has it, or he knows where it is. And once I get my hands on him, believe you me, he'll tell!"

"Just how do you think he could have gotten it the night of the holdup, Louis?" Tamm Oaks kicked a smoldering stick back into the fire. "You're not so strong in your arguments. What you tell of the happenings that night, and what you are asking us to believe about what happened to the money, don't hold together. How could Gage have got any knowledge of your plans, so that he could be on the spot?"

Peele gave Oaks a boring scrutiny, then shrugged, and spoke with the air of a man reluctantly capitulating.

"I think he was acquainted with Vord Creegan, if you must know; that, after Porky and Vord separated, Creegan met Hardin at some appointed place; that Creegan had the cash with him; that he turned the cash box over to Hardin and deliberately let the posse catch him in order to help Hardin get away with the money. Vord thought he would be clever enough to get away from the posse, or break out of jail. He wasn't smart enough for that."

"Hardin, associating with Creegan?" Oaks protested. "Why would he be doing that? I can't see your reasoning, Louis."

"You don't expect me to cry about that, do you?" Peele's face twisted into a sneer, a sneer rendered malevolent by the scrubby new growth of reddish beard on his jaws. "I know what I know. For four years I've been trying to worry Hardin into a mix-up, but he wouldn't draw; for four years I've been trying to get a chance to search that ranch from one end to the other—but I could never manage it. I got tired of shilly-shallying. I'd not be in the mess I'm in now if I hadn't had such weak-kneed fools for men."

"Too bad," sighed Sundquist.

Peele loosed a smooth and rippling flow of curses. "You're plenty right, it's too bad! When I finally decided to stop waiting and act, everything went wrong from the first. Wilder and White had to beat Vandover to a jelly before I could make him agree to baiting Hardin by butchering his horses. I knew that would draw Gage, I know what he thinks of horses. I thought he'd be mad enough to take the whole crew and make a dash after Vandover—and the fool went alone!"

"Didn't leave you much chance to search the ranch while he was gone, did it?" hazarded Oaks.

Peele cursed again. "It *would* have given me time, if he'd left the ranch unguarded as I expected him to. He was doing me no good down there, not all by himself. I had to get him back, and find some other way of clearing the ranch."

"So you killed Lon Pope, and stole Mary Silver," Salt River Charley put in, with utmost casualness, as if slaughter and abduction were commonplace.

"And learned what white-livered men I had in doing it!"

Peele glared at him in fury, remembering. "The only two I could force to help me with both Pope and the girl were Wilder and White. Wilder and White were the only two real men I had—and they're lying back there under the rocks full of the sheriff's bullets, with Red Corcoran on top of them. Blast that fool Doe Gaston! He shot the whole works when he sent for Guy Shawnessy!"

"Too bad!" Sundquist murmured again. "Then you had to run for it, instead of taking Hardin into camp and trying to force him to tell where the money is hidden."

"What could we do but run?" raged Peele. "Instead of having the whole isolated country to ourselves, we get the sheriff on our trail; instead of just having Hardin to cope with, because of something he thinks we did, but could never prove it, we're forced to fire on an officer of the law— and now we *are* in for it. And it's going to take us a long time to get clear, so we can round up Hardin again."

"Yeah. It's going to take a long time and a lot of very crafty planning, Louis."

"Well, I can manage. Why do you think I grabbed the three of you and made you prisoners instead of killing you on the spot? I've told you often enough that I have use for you. There are places in these hills where we can hide so securely that the devil himself couldn't find us. We'll have no trouble staying clear of capture. And once the smoke's blown over, we'll have no trouble drawing Hardin, either." Peele's gaze played among Oaks, Salt River, and Sundquist with unmistakable significance. "And I don't care what I have to do to you three to draw him, either! He's the only living man who knows where that money is."

"What about Bluex, Sidney, and Creegan, sitting there in the pen?" Oaks interrupted. "I thought you were so sure that Creegan knew."

A gleam of some unreadable emotion hardened Peele's already hard eyes.

"You don't know what place that holdup happened in, do you? And I'll never tell you. You don't know what prison those three went to, either. You never will know if you wait to get it from me. But four years ago, there was an attempted prison break in that penitentiary. There wasn't much talk about it. It was nipped in the bud so easily. Five men got away, the prison officers right behind them. One of the five was shot a short way from the prison walls.

"The other four kept going till they got to the edge of a bad marsh, a marsh called Lobo Swamp. That's an ugly swamp, full of sinks as bad as quicksand; nobody ever goes into it intentionally—because those that go into it never come out again. And"—Peele spaced his words to give them grim meaning—"the four escaping convicts—trying to lose the officers behind them—dashed into Lobo Swamp."

"Hell's fire!" ejaculated Oaks.

"I thought that would make you sit up. The officers weren't fools enough to try to follow, they knew they didn't have to. They simply stood on the bank of the swamp and waited till the convicts stuck in the mud, then they shot them down like rats in a trap, and left them there to rot. And— three of the four were George Sidney, Jean Bluex, and— Vord Creegan. *I'm* the only man of that gang left alive. Hardin is the only man left alive who knows where the money is. And I'll trail him to hell and back again, but I'll find out where he put it and get it away from him!"

No one answered him. He became silent, staring into the fire, thinking of that disastrous day, four years past, when five men had tried to break from prison.

CHAPTER XII

LOBO SWAMP

THAT had been a day of hope for those five men. They had planned the break for seven weeks. They had everything ready that morning; they failed to see how their plot could go awry. The plans worked just far enough then to shoot down a guard and succeed in getting outside the prison wall. The one who had killed the guard was shot down, and the four remaining dashed away with the wail of the siren following them.

When they reached the edge of the swamp, they rushed into it without a moment's hesitation. They *did* know the character of the swamp, but no chance was too desperate— they knew the prison officers would not follow them there.

Within a very few seconds they knew how hopelessly they had trapped themselves. Officers' guns spoke from the bank. The convicts went down into the mud and slime, mercifully dead, saved the ghastly horrors of death in the swamp—all but one.

That one felt the thud of a bullet in his side, and deliberately threw himself face downward in the mud. He held his breath as the water closed over him. He had planned this thing to the last detail, he had even aimed his course minutely as he plunged into the swamp.

He was the man whom Hardin had described as a "big, ugly bruiser called Vord Creegan."

He lay there in the mud and water till his lungs seemed bursting with the punishment of holding his breath. He felt in the slime for the brush clump toward which he had steered his feet.

His hand grasped one grimy stem. He drew himself

toward it, slowly turning his body over, until his head touched the brush beneath the water. He lifted his face till his nose was above water. Carefully and slowly he let the air out of his lungs, and took another breath.

He could hear nothing. The shooting from the bank had ceased. He could see nothing. He was keeping his eyes closed against the foul waters of the swamp. He raised one hand cautiously along the brush stem. His fingers came into contact with slime-coated leaves. He raised his hand still a little higher. He felt it reach the surface of the water, more twigs, and a thick clump of leaves.

He drew his hand down, and reached on through the water directly beyond his head. Numerous brush stems were there, growing closely together. He drew his body onward till his head was among the stems of brush. Then he raised his head till his face was above the water's surface and opened his eyes.

The slime in his eyes nearly blinded him, but he could discern enough to see that his head was hidden by the brush, his body hidden by the water. He raised one cautious hand to his face and wiped the fetid ooze from his eyes. He raised his face a little higher still, in order to peer between the leaves and twigs of the brush. The prison officers were sitting on the bank, watching the swamp. Creegan turned his head to look around. The other three men had sunk below the surface—the ooze and slime were tinged thickly with a dark, dingy red.

He alone lived out of that break. The wound in his side was stinging from the effect of the water and mud. He lay motionless, beginning to shiver from the chill of the swamp.

What seemed an age passed; the chill bit into him, sinking through his flesh till even his bones seemed cold. And still the prison officers sat on the bank, watching, to be certain that not one of the four escaped men was alive.

The convict began to wonder how long he could hold out.

As the torturing hours lengthened, he began to grow numb. He forced his mind from thoughts of the officers there a short distance beyond him, and focused it desperately on one vital thought—he *had* to live; no one but he knew where that iron box lay with its contents of seventy-five one-thousand-dollar bills. He had to live!

He set his teeth against the agony of the numbing chill and looked up at the sun. The hour must be close to four o'clock. Another four hours and it would be dark. He set himself to endure. The numbness began to creep into his head.

He thought once that he was in the hills at the scene of the holdup, that he heard Louis Peele's voice shouting: "Vord! Porky! Somebody stop that fool—get that box!" Well, he'd gotten it. He chuckled foolishly, then shook himself clear-brained in a wave of panic, realizing that he had all but lost consciousness.

He looked toward the bank. The light was fading. The officers were gone. The trees and hills stood in clear outline against the sunset sky. The swamp brooded in solitude over its dead.

He gathered his failing forces of sensibility and strength. The time had come to move on. He tried to take his hands from the brush stems. They were so numbed that they were like hands frozen to what they grasped. He set his teeth against pain, and began striving to work his hands free.

They loosened their grip, a finger at a time. He lifted them out of the water and tried to work them together, sitting upright for the first time since he had entered the swamp. So sitting, the water reached up to his chin.

He persisted working at his hands, clenching his teeth, and twice he could not suppress a groan at the pain the effort cost him. The sluggish blood began to circulate more rapidly, the blue hands began to turn red with returning life. He extended his efforts to his arms. There seemed to be no life in them.

By the time he got them live enough that they felt more like arms than limbs of stone, there was only a last lingering glow in the sky, the trees and hills had turned as black as the swamp. He tried to get to his feet, but his numb body would not answer the behest of his brain.

He struggled to his knees, and the level of the swamp sank to his chest. He reached down through the water and worked at his thighs, his calves. By the time he had forced an answering pain there, there was only a shade left between dusk and the night. He examined the skyline, and chose for landmark a tree silhouetted in the moonlight, and in whose direction the bank was nearest.

Summoning all the strength at his command, he managed to rise to his feet. Staggering and stumbling like a drunken man, he started toward the bank. About a third of the way to the bank, stumbling, falling, dragging himself erect again, he struck the edge of one of those treacherous sinks.

The mud sucked at his left foot. For an instant wild fear paralyzed his muscles, then with a frantic effort he pulled the foot free and lurched to the right. The effort threw him on his face in the mud. He fought like a madman to gain his feet, and went on.

A little way farther, he struck another sink. That time he thought he was gone. He fought terror and sink together. He dragged one foot free, only to find the other caught. He dragged that one free, to find himself down on all fours.

He thrashed at the mud in insane panic. His very fury threw him clear of the sink. He half lay in the mud and water, breathing in gasps, for several minutes, before he could call on his last reserve of strength and drag himself upright again.

He was close to the edge of hysteria, from the frightful strain, the protracted exposure and pain. He stood swaying in water up to his knees, and began his lurching advance again. He staggered on for several yards, felt his foot strike something hard, and fell forward on his face.

He was barely conscious of what he was doing. He lay supine for several moments, striving to clear his brain. He raised his head and stared about. The moon was very bright. It had been in the sky before the sun went down. Now it was like a guiding light. Weak with relief at what he saw, he dropped his head on his arms and sobbed aloud. He had reached the bank.

CHAPTER XIII

DRIFTING COWBOY

HE remained there till he felt himself shivering anew with the chill of the swamp, his mucked clothes sticking to his cold skin. Then his brain began to function clearly again. He struggled to his feet, fell prone, and once more staggered to an upright position. Weaving from side to side, threatening with every step to fall on his face, he began to walk.

Gradually the lurching shamble turned to steadier locomotion. The more swiftly circulating blood began to warm his body. And suddenly he no longer staggered or weaved. His footsteps quickened. He began to run. The run was awkward, but it grew less awkward quickly, he warmed perceptibly. He continued running till his shortened breath forced him to slow to a walk once more.

It was just then that he heard the dog bark. It was barking as dogs often do bark, apparently for the fun of it.

He sighed in relief. "Where there's a dog, there are people," he said to himself, turned at an angle, and tramped wearily toward the sound. "I'll have to go damn carefully," he reminded himself. "I dare not be seen. All I want is some place where I can filch a little food from some field."

The dog continued to bark, at intervals, like a sentinel placed there to guide the man trudging onward. Because of his confusing weariness and tired brain, he did not realize how close he was drawing toward the sound, till a new note entered the animal's voice. The dog was abruptly barking not for fun, but because it smelled and heard something that caught its attention.

The convict shook himself to alert observance and staggered to a halt—too late. He had stumbled into a small clearing, and he saw a man in range garb spring erect in the bright moonlight.

"Halt right there!" A peremptory command assailed his ears. "Who are you and what do you want?"

The fugitive choked back a gasp of dismay. With that dog to trail him, any attempt at escape would be futile. He did the only thing left him to do—he answered, and his voice was a mere hoarse croak.

"Let me come up and explain. I'm lost. Lost, hungry, done up."

"All right, come ahead. Shut up, Shep!"

The dog had sunk his bark to a threatening growl. He ceased even that, and slunk to his master's feet.

The fugitive advanced, striving to command his whirling brain, lurched, clutched wildly at the air, and fell in a heap.

The man leaped forward with an alarmed ejaculation and bent over him. He was unconscious. The man bending above him passed a hand along the convict's side, and muttered in astonishment:

"Wet to the hide! Get out of the way, Shep! We have to build a fire."

When the fire was going well, and he had dragged the unconscious man closer to it, he saw by the light of the flames the prison clothes, the shaved head, the drying mud of the swamp. Investigating, he found the wound in the convict's side.

Often when a dog is hurt, cut, bitten by a snake, if there is mud available, the dog will crawl into it, impelled by instinct to seek a healing agency. Something in the mud and water does the trick. Dogs know. The cowboy knew dogs. The wound in the man's side was superficial; that mud would take care of it. It was no more than a long score in the flesh.

The cowboy sat back on his heels and stared at the senseless man. He was still sitting there when the fugitive stirred and awoke in the early morning, opened his eyes and looked at the man watching him from across the fire.

"You're one of the jaspers who got away from the big pen yesterday, aren't you?" the cowboy asked without preamble.

"Yes." The convict sat up, his face cold and expressionless. "I went into the swamp. The officers shot at us. I threw myself down, lay there until dark, and got out. If you— if you make any try———"

"Drop it," the cowboy interrupted. "I don't care who you are or what you did to get yourself into prison, I wouldn't raise a finger to send you back. I was in a pen once—uh— to see a friend. You can forget that. There's a creek right there beyond that clump of trees. You can wash in it. I'm just camped here with my horse and dog. On my way to a line camp. I have an extra shirt and an extra pair of jeans with me. Take 'em, and welcome.

"We'll burn those things you have on. You can have my hat; I've another at the line camp. Sorry I haven't any extra boots. You'll have to go barefooted. You can have my socks, though. I don't need 'em. You don't dare keep anything you brought out of that place with you. And you can have my pack horse. I'll take my kit on the back of my saddle. I'd give you my saddle horse, but he's branded. The pack horse isn't. Fair enough?"

The convict drew a deep breath, then began awkwardly to voice his gratitude.

The cowboy cut short his thanks. "Better get moving," he said gruffly.

Two days later, a man wearing an old black Stetson hat, a faded flannel shirt, and a pair of jeans, in his sock feet, rode a fat little plug of a pack horse through the hills, traveling by night. He came within three days to a seldom-used line cabin to which the cowboy had directed him, subsisting during the journey on a meager supply of bread and beans furnished him by the same cowboy. The wound in the rider's side was healing rapidly. It had given him no trouble. At the old cabin he found food, shelter, a place to rest—and let his hair grow.

Just about a month later, the same man rode the fat pack horse to an isolated ranch. He said he was named "Chuck" Weaver. He said he had fallen asleep too close to his campfire, had burned his boots and been forced to throw them away. He was looking for a job. The season was nearing round-up time. The foreman of the ranch hired him.

One of the men loaned him an extra pair of boots till pay day. He worked through the round-up, traded his pack horse for a saddle horse, giving money enough to boot for full value, and faded from the scene of the ranch, leaving no more memory behind him than that of Chuck Weaver, drifting cowboy, one of the several who came by every year.

His general course lay toward a town named Tenville. He wore his dark, curling hair rather long, as if he had a secret aversion to very short hair. He wore a short, curling beard. He worked when he needed money, and moved on. He reached Tenville. Cautious inquiry elicited the information that Louis Peele had long been gone from that territory, and no man knew where he might be.

The entire country had changed; old-timers had moved away, newcomers had moved in. Few remembered Louis Peele, save as a wild yearling who had almost got himself into trouble by associating with bad companions.

Chuck Weaver rode on. Four years passed before he finally located Louis Peele in Great Lost Valley. But when he reached Great Lost Valley, Louis Peele was gone. Weaver rode on to the next ranch, left his horse standing in the yard, and went up to the house to make inquiry. He knocked upon the back door.

CHAPTER XIV

ON THE TRAIL

THE door swung open to disclose a tall, rugged, good-looking blond man. The blond man smiled a perfunctory welcome.

"My name is Chuck Weaver." Weaver surveyed the blond man with covert scrutiny. "I am trying to find an old friend of mine. I have found his ranch deserted. I came over here to ask after him. I reckon that you, living on the next ranch, might know where he's gone. I'm looking for Louis Peele."

The blond man's face betrayed no least change of expression. "I don't live here, Chuck Weaver. I can tell you nothing about Louis Peele. I am Guy Shawnessy, sheriff of this county. This ranch is the Circle Crossbar, owned by Gage Hardin. He is not around right now."

The shot told, as Shawnessy had expected it to do.

The man who called himself Weaver caught his breath, and one gasp of consternation escaped him. Then he commanded himself into quick control, and all expression died out of his face. "Thank you, sheriff. I won't trouble you further." He turned and went back to his horse with a rapid stride.

Doe Gaston and Mary Silver were just coming across the yard toward the house. They watched Weaver curiously as he mounted and rode away. Mary looked up at the sheriff standing in the doorway as she and Doe ascended the back steps.

"Who was that, Guy? What did he want?"

Shawnessy frowned, pursing his lips dubiously. "He said his name was Chuck Weaver, Mary. He was looking for Louis Peele. He said that Louis was an old friend of his."

Doe Gaston stopped short on the top step. "That's it! I

knew he looked like somebody I'd seen. He looks like Peele! He looks enough like him to be his brother."

"I noticed it," Shawnessy replied quietly. "Chuck Weaver, eh? Well, Doc, I'd give a good deal to know what he wants of Peele—and what his name may be; I would wager anything you want to specify that Chuck Weaver isn't it."

"He gave me the creeps!" Mary Silver repressed a shiver. "There was something sinister about him, something brooding, deadly, ready to spring. He looked like—like——"

"He looked like a man who had been through several hells," Shawnessy furnished the words she struggled to find. "I studied him closely during the short time he was standing there before me. He can't possibly *be* Peele's brother. Harry Peele is dead, there can be no mistake about that; Gage saw Harry's body there with the body of his brother Bruce. No, Weaver can't be Peele's brother. But who is he? If I'd had the least excuse for it, I'd have held him. I had none."

"If he's a friend of Peele, if he had anything to do with that holdup, for instance," said Doc slowly, "where's he been all these years? Why wait all this time to hunt Peele up again?"

"I'd give a good horse to know, Doc."

Shawnessy turned from the doorway and walked back into the room. Mary and Doc followed him.

"Men sometimes get out of prison," the sheriff went on. "That *could* be the answer."

Doc shook his head. "I don't see how. They were all shot down in that swamp. I told you that. Gage and I read it in the papers; there wasn't much said about it."

"This thing here is getting better." Shawnessy touched his stiff arm. "I'm getting stronger. In a few days more I'll be out of here and on the trail. And if Chuck Weaver follows the wake of Louis Peele, I'll know it."

* * * *

But it was Gage Hardin who overtook sign of Louis Peele first. And it was Chuck Weaver who overtook Hardin first. He overtook him the night before Hardin went into Loody's store to ask for food. When Hardin came out of Loody's store and rode away, he little dreamed that every move he and Loody had made had been watched, every word spoken between them overheard, that when he went on he was followed by a big, bearded man who rode a coal-black horse.

When Hardin lay down to sleep that night in a canyon, Chuck Weaver was close enough to watch all he did, to mark the direction of his course. That ascertained, Weaver rode on.

When Louis Peele sat at the campfire arguing with Oaks, Sundquist, and Salt River Charley, Weaver lay concealed so close to them that he could hear every syllable spoken between them. When Peele and his men broke camp and moved on, Weaver followed, far enough behind to escape detection, close enough to miss no move that was made by the fugitive band. When Peele and his men camped again at daylight, Weaver stood hidden on a ridge staring down at them.

"The same old Louis," he muttered to himself. "The same old Louis, with his sharp dark eyes, his heavy dark hair, with the reddish beard and his dudish looks. Not a soul there that I know but Peele," Weaver mused. "I had better go slow. There is no telling what the rest of them know, no telling what this whole maneuver is about. I didn't get much information out of Sheriff Shawnessy, or anybody else. I'll have to keep on going slow and lying low till I get my bearings—unless I want to run the risk of being sent back to the pen. And you can be sure that they'll never take me back there unless they take me feet first!"

CHAPTER XV

A BIT OF NEWS

SHAWNESSY, Mary Silver, and Doe Gaston were at breakfast when Jefferson Baker rode into the yard, dismounted, and came into the house to see how the sheriff's condition was improving.

"The stiffness is going fast." And Shawnessy lifted his arm to prove it. "I can't stay around here any longer, Jeff. I have to go."

"You'll not go under another week!" Baker answered sharply. "You are weaker than you realize. You'll find that out when you begin riding. Do as I tell you to do and you may be able to travel within another week, certainly not before. I have some queer news for you three."

"Have you heard from Gage?" Doe demanded, leaning forward in eagerness.

"Indirectly, Doe. It looks as if Hardin were pretty hard run. A fellow named Casper Loody, who keeps a general store at some godforsaken place called Elks Crossing, had a visit from Hardin three nights ago. From what Loody said, Hardin held him up, demanded food, said he had no money, and would pay later. He frightened the wits out of Loody. He told Loody what he was in that country for, but Loody didn't believe him."

"Where did you hear this?" Shawnessy cut in.

Baker bit his lip, and a frown darkened his face.

"I heard it from a rider Loody sent down here. Funny thing. According to Loody, Hardin hadn't been gone two minutes when another man walked into the store, a man Loody described as being every bit as big as Hardin, wearing a gun and a short beard.

"He told Loody that if he wanted to report the holdup he could get word to the sheriff at the Circle Crossbar Ranch in Great Lost Valley. He also told Loody that he had an idea the sheriff would still be at the Circle Crossbar all right, that the sheriff's left arm had seemed a little stiff, that he had looked pale and weak, as if he might be recovering from an illness—or a wound."

"Chuck Weaver!" ejaculated Shawnessy. "He managed to see a good deal in the minute he stood here facing me, didn't he?"

"Who's Chuck Weaver?" Baker inquired.

"That's what we'd all like to know!" Shawnessy laughed, a laugh that contained more of anger than mirth. "He came here a few days ago looking for Louis Peele. He answers the description Loody gave, all right. But—holding up a store, Jeff! I wish Gage hadn't been compelled to do that."

"A man has to eat!" Doe defended the absent Gage. "If he had merely asked for the grub, he might not have got it. Did he draw a gun on the fellow?"

"I suppose so," Baker answered. "Loody said he 'held me up.'"

"Well, it's bad business." Shawnessy turned hard eyes on Baker. "Arm or no arm, weak or not, I'm getting out of here before Gage plunges himself into a bad mess."

"Not until next week you don't go!" Baker said curtly. "Even that's altogether too soon for you to be making a ride like that. I've told you so."

Shawnessy got to his feet, face and voice eloquent of impatience.

"I'm leaving tonight."

"You are not!" Baker rose, angry and excited. "You're not leaving till next week. You'll break yourself down and have a relapse if you start a day sooner. You can leave next week, if I can't hold you any longer. And I'm going with you."

"Thanks. I was going to ask you to. But you don't hold me a day longer than next week, so don't try it. I have to see this Loody. This business is getting worse every hour."

Shawnessy sat down abruptly, shaken by his excitement and perturbation, realizing that he was still a pretty weak man.

CHAPTER XVI

THREE FROM TEN

Upon the night of that same day, Everett Finley, another isolated keeper of a small store far back in the lonely mountains was directing his son, nicknamed "Rusty," in shelving some goods that had come in by stage the day before to the town ten miles away, been brought on to him by wagon. Both had their backs turned to the door, when a harsh voice broke the silence of the small, cluttered room.

"Put up your hands and turn around!"

They whirled about, sixty-year-old Finley and his nineteen-year-old son, to see a man advancing into the room, a leveled gun in either hand. Finley's gaze leaped over the intruder in swift, startled survey—a big man, well over six feet tall, with dark hair and eyes, dark mustache, and a short, square black beard.

"What do you want?" Finley demanded, and shot a harried glance at his son. Rusty's temper was inflammable and unmanageable. Under his breath Finley commanded sharply: "You keep still, Rusty, and don't make any wild moves." Then he said again to the man with the guns: "What do you want?"

"I want nothing but food," the big man answered. "I am not holding you up. I am trailing an escaped murderer, and I have run out of money and food. I am inviting you to stake me to the food, and make it quick."

"I haven't heard of any escaped murderer up this way," Finley replied. "But we don't get news very fast or often. You may be telling the truth."

"I *am* telling the truth. Don't waste time talking. Get me the food, and I'll go on and let you alone. My name is

Hardin, Gage Hardin. I'll send the money for whatever you furnish me, later. I'd appreciate the loan of a few dollars, also."

"You get——" Rusty began hotly.

"I told you to keep your mouth shut!" Finley cut him short. "You get the man five dollars out of the till, and I'll get him some grub."

Rusty backed to the counter, muttering his rebellion in a savage undertone. He saw himself as a potential hero, who might win flattering praises afterward for having used his brilliant wits to save his father's goods from a holdup man. He did not believe a word that man had told his father. As Finley walked to the shelf a few feet from where he had been standing, to secure some ready edible foods, Rusty passed around the end of the counter and paused before the cash drawer built into the counter.

His father kept a small gun in that drawer. Rusty jerked the drawer open and snatched up the gun.

The man just inside the doorway saw the youth's hand come out of the drawer bearing the small revolver. The gun in the man's right hand crashed, and Rusty dropped, a bullet in his head.

Finley whirled, crying out in horror. In one hand he held a slab of cheese. He hurled it madly at the man across the counter. It struck the man's right shoulder, but it could not act either as deterrent or confuse his aim. As he threw the cheese, Finley started to leap over the counter. The other leveled gun crashed, and Finley hurtled to the floor, a bullet tearing through his body.

The man with the guns glared down at him in fury. "Why didn't you give me what I wanted peaceably? Why did you lose your head and force me to fire?"

Finley lay still. The other man holstered his guns, caught up an armful of foodstuffs, and dashed out of the store.

Everett Finley opened his eyes, glazed eyes that stared

madly after the disappearing marauder. "Oh, God!" Finley prayed silently. "Let somebody get here in time!" He tried to draw himself up, but there was no strength left in him. He tried to cry loudly, "Rusty!" Blood bubbled in his throat and clouded his utterance.

But Rusty was beyond ever hearing anything again, no matter how loud or diminished the tone.

Down the road twisting through the trees, several hundred yards away, "Swede" Thoburn, yawning with weariness, had just gone to bed. He heard the sound of revolver reports, in the direction of the store. He leaped out of bed, jerked on his boots in the dark, and rushed out of his rough one-room shack. Through the night, between the boles of the trees, he could catch a spark of light that was the hanging kerosene lamp in the store.

Swede stood staring for a moment, transfixed, then started up the twisting, narrow road at a wild run. As he reached the open door of the store, only one step above the ground, he jerked himself to a halt, grasping loudly at sight of Finley lying on the floor with blood bubbling from his lips.

Finley's dulled eyes barely discerned him there, thick-chested Swede Thoburn in his undershirt and long drawers.

"Swede!" he choked. "Swede!"

"Yah!" In one spring Swede reached him and knelt beside him. "Finley! Who did it?"

"A holdup—Swede." Finley groped at his choking throat. "He said his—name—was Gage Hardin. Big man—black hair—black beard—square. Rusty! Swede! Rusty—behind the—counter——" Finley's eyes rolled upward. The blood in his throat smothered his voice.

Swede wet his lips, staring down at Finley's body in a trance of horror, and he was not a sight for mirth in his old boots and underwear, blood on his hands and knees. He turned his face away, blundering toward the door.

He had to dress and rouse somebody. He couldn't think

yet who it would be. There was no one else living near the store, only Mrs. Finley. He gulped at the thought of having to tell Mrs. Finley.

As he lurched blindly out of the door, he almost ran into a man advancing toward the door. He lifted his dazed gaze, and his eyes bulged. Words of Finley's sounded in his ears —"big man—black hair—black beard——"

"You!" Swede gasped, doubling his fists.

The big man thrust forward a deterring hand. "Easy, mister! I didn't do it. I tried to get here in time to stop it. I was too late. I stepped back out of sight as I saw you go in. Send somebody for the sheriff. You'll find him at the Circle Crossbar Ranch, in Great Lost Valley."

"Where's that?" asked Swede.

"About a hundred miles south and west from here, see? Get word to him, quick. I'm after the fellow who did the shooting."

"Who are you?" demanded Swede bluntly.

"Chuck Weaver is the name, mister. I have to ride. You get the sheriff."

Weaver darted out of sight, into the night. Swede, as he ran toward his shack and his clothes, heard the sound of furiously departing hoofs.

Several miles beyond the Finley store, Louis Peele and his men sat grouped close to a low campfire, talking. To the most casual eye, had there been any eye to observe them, they were all tense with excitement.

Tamm Oaks, hunched in his jacket, buttoned all the way up to his throat, looked up at Peele from beneath lowering brows. "I don't see through your maneuver, Louis. But whatever it is, I don't like it. We finally manage to begin on a few hours' sleep, and you kick us awake and tell us we have to travel."

"And when I say travel, that's what I mean!" Peele was holding himself in leash with visible difficulty. "While you were all asleep, I rode back to see whether I could get a sight of Hardin. We don't dare let him get too close. I want no fight with him now! I saw nothing till I came within view of the dinky store where you and Fitz went in to buy some stuff yesterday. There were three men and a woman there. The men were in a rage, the woman was crying. I got near enough to hear what was being said. Maybe you'll believe what I've been telling you, now. Your friend Hardin has broken loose, at last."

"What!" Sundquist roused, just beyond Oaks.

Oaks felt carefully and slyly of his side, then he loosened the button at his throat, as if he were too warm. The men had grown used to that movement. Oaks always wore his jacket, and he was always sitting too close to the fire and getting too warm. Oaks had counted on that reaction.

Peele was not looking at Oaks. He was staring at Sundquist.

"I told you he'd do it," Peele went on, his voice lowering in tone and gaining speed. "I stayed there and listened till I learned just what had happened. One of the fellows they called Swede was doing most of the talking. The other men lived somewhere back in the canyons; this Swede had brought them in. The woman was the storekeeper's wife. Hardin had held up the store, had shot and killed the owner and his nineteen-year-old son. I told you Gage would break loose and show himself for what he was, if we led him on far enough."

"Good work!" exclaimed Fitz Tracy. "Another job or two like that and his friend Shawnessy will be on his trail!"

Oaks suddenly straightened and got to his feet. He had loosened more buttons till his jacket front was wide open.

"You're a liar, Louis," he said, very quietly. "Hardin could never do a thing like that!"

"Take it easy, Oaks." Fitz sprang erect, facing Oaks. "One more word out of you and I'll knock you silly."

"Try it and you'll get what you're not looking for!" Oaks stood motionless.

The other men about the fire sat like statues. Dutch Sundquist and Salt River Charley might have been carved out of dark stone. Either of them could have reached out and touched Tamm Oaks, they were so close to him. Peele laughed.

"You'd better cool down, Tamm. Fitz is no man to fool with."

"I'm not fooling," retorted Tamm Oaks. "Fitz is a traitor. He would double-cross you for a plugged nickel. On the way to the store yesterday he told me he was simply waiting a chance to get you unaware."

"That's a lie!" roared Fitz. He dashed down a hand to draw his gun.

Half of Peele's men leaped to their feet. Not in time to save Fitz. From under his open jacket, Tamm Oaks drew a gun. He fired point-blank into Fitz's stomach. As Fitz went down, and Peele's crew turned their fire on Oaks, Oaks managed to fire again, twice.

Finny Hogan went down, both of Oak's bullets in his chest. Four of Peele's men fired in the same instant. Oaks took all four of the bullets. He went down in a swaying, wilting heap. The four who had shot him grouped over him, and Peele ordered them back.

"Get back. He's finished. You other two"—his gaze swept over Dutch Sundquist and Salt River Charley—"don't make a move."

Neither of them looked at him. They stared straight ahead, over the motionless body of Tamm Oaks. Fitz groaned.

"Shut up!" Peele snapped at him. "Where did that fool get a gun?"

None answered.

In a last gasp, Oaks whispered: "Salty—I got—*two.*"

Salt River made no sign. But he had heard. A little muscle quivered over one of his eyes. He was counting to himself. There had been ten of them. Tamm Oaks, Finny Hogan, and Fitz Tracy were done. Three from ten leaves seven. Peele didn't count. They were leaving Louis Peele for Hardin.

Salt River seemed unable to command any other idea. Three from ten leaves seven. The thought rolled around in his head like a ball gone wild on a roulette wheel. Three from ten—he heard Peele spitting commands.

"Weeny, you and Soapy go over there under that tree where the earth's soft and dig a hole. Finny and Oaks are already dead. Fitz will be dead before you get the hole dug. And hurry. We have to move. You'd better help them, Cooky. The rest of us will stay here and keep an eye on Dutch and Charley. Get going."

As the three he had delegated to the task passed from the firelight, Peele turned his attention to the two men sitting as still as if they were as dead as Tamm Oaks.

"Are you two going to keep your heads, or are you going to go wild, as Oaks did?"

Salt River Charley turned a stone-cold gaze on him. "Do we look loco, Louis? I'm afraid Tamm was something of a fool. He was always making trouble. I'm wasting no sympathy on him. Don't think Dutch and I are going to commit suicide as he did. Am I right, Dutch?"

"I would damn well say so." Sundquist's voice was dry. "If we want to save our hides, it would seem the wisest thing to play with Louis."

Peele shrugged. "Correct. Once Hardin runs wild enough, Shawnessy will be after him. I think this last job of his will drag Shawnessy into action. He may be weak yet— I got him several times. But he'll think duty is stronger than life or friendship—he'll hit the trail when he hears of this, or I miss my guess. If you two keep your heads, I may not need you to draw Hardin. I might even let you go in the end. If Hardin does enough to make Shawnessy start after him, things will be working our way."

"How?" asked Sundquist.

"Well, if Shawnessy starts after him, he'll get him. He'll forget us, for the time being. Friendship won't stand in the way of Shawnessy. Once he gets Hardin in jail, we will slip in and promise Hardin we'll get him out—if he'll tell us where the seventy-five thousand is cached. Oh, yes, things may be working our way very soon, if we simply lay low and lead Gage on."

"Are you going to be soft enough to let Hardin in on the split if you do succeed in getting the money?" inquired Salt River Charley.

"Do I look like an idiot?" Peele counter-questioned. "Once we get Hardin out of jail, and he either takes us to the money, or tells us where it is—split with him? Hardly! We will bury him so deep he'll never come up again."

The dying Fitz groaned again, and Peele turned on him.

"Shut up, Fitz!" He shrugged and commented to Salt River: "He's dying fast. He'll be dead in another ten minutes."

He was. And Tamm Oaks, Finny Hogan, and Fitz Tracy were all buried in the same shallow hole, covered with rocks, and left there together under the stars, as the remaining seven rode with Peele on into the night. They rode silently, save for the few whispered words that passed between Dutch Sundquist and Salt River Charley.

"Do you know where he got the gun, Charley?"

"Yes. Didn't he tell you?"

"No."

"It was your gun, Dutch. He managed to get hold of it when Hogan wasn't looking, yesterday."

"Oh. Well, he took two. I hope we can do that good."

"So do I, Dutch. You get anything yet?"

"No. Have you?"

"Yes. That hunting knife Cooky has been using to cut potatoes and open cans. He thinks he lost it. I'm no good with a knife. I'll give it to you."

"Good boy, Charley. I'll get something, soon."

"Let me know when you do, Dutch."

"Sure. Charley, three from ten leaves——"

"Leaves seven," finished Salt River Charley.

The seven rode on, Peele at their head. They had no need to ride very far. Havens for the pursued were many there in the uninhabited fastness of the wilds.

A distance to the rear of them, close enough to follow their general direction and far enough to escape their detection, rode a large man on a coal-black horse. Frequently the following man turned to glance back and scan the terrain behind him in the moonlit darkness.

"If they keep this up," he told himself as he trailed them, "I'll be able to get Peele by himself before long. A few more upsets like this, and it won't be long. No, it won't be long."

CHAPTER XVII

Doe Gaston rose in the middle of the night to answer loud knocking on the back door of the ranch house. He lighted the lamp and swung open the door to find there on the porch Long Lister, a cowboy from the Diamond W Ranch. Lister was disheveled and importunate. He pushed into the room with little ceremony the moment Gaston unlocked the door.

"What's up now?" demanded Doe, quick alarm running through him at Lister's appearance.

Lister glanced across the room to the cot bed where the sheriff lay. Shawnessy was wide awake, gazing at him with intent interest, as Lister answered Doe's question.

"A fellow just rode in from the north, Doe. Hardin's gone wild. He held up a little store back in the hills, killed the storekeeper—a man named Finley—and Finley's nineteen-year-old son. The fellow tried to telegraph us, but the lines were still out and he came on in without wasting time. I wish we lived in more civilized country. Imagine Gage breaking loose like that."

"I was afraid of it!" Shawnessy sat erect in his bed.

Mary Silver threw open her door and moved quickly into the room.

"I don't believe it!" she said. "I can't believe it."

"Certainly not!" Doe breathed heavily. "They always exaggerate these things. Gage never killed anybody. There's a crazy twist somewhere. You ought to know Gage better than to believe such a report, Long."

"I'm sorry, Doe." Lister's eyes were harried with distress. "But there seems to be no doubt of it. The fellow who came after the sheriff gave me all the particulars. I brought

103

him with me. He's waiting in the yard. I'll bring him in, and you can hear what he has to say for yourself. Shall I?"

"Certainly. Bring him in immediately!" said Mary. "We *must* hear what he has to say. Go get him, Long."

"Yes'm." Long stepped to the door, pulled it open, and called: "Will you come in, Swede? They're all waiting to hear your account of the holdup."

Heavy steps ascended the back steps in answer, crossed the porch, and Swede Thoburn halted just inside the door, apparently startled at the sight of Mary Silver. He had not expected to find a woman there. Her presence confused him and stayed his tongue. Swede was unused to the association of women, and the thing he had to tell did not seem to him fit for a woman's ears. He had to force himself to speak.

When he had finished, Shawnessy was sitting erect in bed, his gaze carefully averted from Mary's face.

"Just when did this happen?" he asked.

"Five nights ago, sheriff," Swede answered. "Ay left next morning. Ay come by horse and stage."

"I see. Was there anybody else around the store?"

No, Swede replied, there had been nobody there but Finley. Not until after the shooting. There was then the big man he had seen as he started out the door, the big man who had said his name was Chuck Weaver and who had told Swede where to find the sheriff. That, Swede concluded, was quite all.

"Gage didn't do it," Mary said steadily, standing by the head of the bed gripping Shawnessy's uninjured arm with tense fingers. "He *couldn't* do anything like that."

"Not he," Doe agreed stanchly. "There's some insane mistake somewhere."

Long Lister cleared his throat. He was vastly uncomfortable, but he had the support that upholds a man when he is certain he is in the right. "Mistake? I don't see how there can be any mistake, Doe. He said his name was Gage

Hardin. Finley, dying gave that information to Thoburn. Can you see any room for error, Guy?"

"Guess not, Long. But since that was all Finley lived to tell, we can't know what happened. Very likely Gage merely asked for food, as he did at Elks Crossing. Finley may have been an excitable person, he may have thought Gage was trying to hold him up and snatched a gun from under the counter or something of the sort, forcing Hardin to shoot in self-defense."

"Finley wasn't like that," Swede said earnestly. "He never got excited. Ay know him for years. If anybody got excited, it was Rusty. He got mad at nothing, yust like that."

"Well, it may have been the boy who started the shooting, then," said Shawnessy. "There are a hundred possibilities, and we haven't much to go on. We may know more when we get there. We will leave tomorrow morning at daybreak. It doesn't matter what Baker says, we're going. Would you know this man who told you he was Chuck Weaver again, Thoburn?"

Swede was vehement. "Ay sure vould. Ay know that faller in hal!"

"I believe you said he had a black beard, too, didn't you?"

Swede nodded. "He sure did."

Shawnessy turned to Doe Gaston. "Doe, take Thoburn in to sleep with you, so he can be fit to travel again in the morning. I have a good many things to accomplish; right now, I want to talk to Mary, alone."

A vast and troubled irresolution held Gaston motionless and tongue-tied; the misery that weighed him down emanated from him like something tangible, but there was nothing any one could say to alleviate it.

Long Lister cleared his throat, having grown intolerably uneasy in the lengthening silence. "Anything I—anything more I can do?"

Doe seemed suddenly to increase in spiritual stature. His

shoulders straightened, his head lifted, his indecision vanished. "Yes, there is, Long. Before you go home, ride on up to the J Bar B and tell Jeff Baker to be here by daybreak. Tell him that Guy is leaving then, that the latest developments make it impossible for any of us to try to hold him here any longer."

"Sure, glad to. I'll go straight there." Lister's eagerness to be of some use carried him across the room in a brisk stride. He turned his head to call back as he went out the door: "So long, everybody."

No one answered him, but he was gone so quickly that he never knew it.

Doe Gaston's world was in chaos, but his feet were grounded firmly, on something he would have called a hybrid of faith and horse sense, had he stopped to analyze it. He did not look at Shawnessy. He addressed his speech and attention to Mary Silver alone.

"Gage never did it—we're believing that blindly, until Gage himself gives us the lie to our faith. Come along, Thoburn; you need to get some sleep."

He went from the room, the weary Thoburn at his heels. As the door to the bedroom closed behind them, Shawnessy gestured to the chair beside the head of his bed.

"Come over here and sit down, Mary. I suppose any words I can get out will prove useless, but there are some things that I want to try to say."

Mary advanced to the bed and seated herself on the edge of the chair. There was about her the air of something poised for startled flight.

"You have already decided that Gage is guilty, haven't you, Guy? I can see it in your face."

Shawnessy reached out his right hand and gripped both of hers, where they lay crossed in her lap.

"You can't see anything of that sort in my face, Mary— because I have made no such decision. I have made no decision at all. It isn't impossible that Gage should be guilty. We've gone all over that before, his temper, his hard determination, the near frenzy into which he might be driven should something threaten to balk him of seeing Louis Peele get his just deserts at last. You know the strength of the friendship that has existed between Gage and me. You know my capacity for loyalty. Don't you?"

"Yes, yes, of course. But I——"

"But you must not lose sight of the fact that I am not my own man. I am the sheriff, Mary. I dare not dismiss the possibility that Gage *may* be guilty."

"Yes." Mary rose to her feet, laying one hand on his uninjured arm. "I'll go. Good night, Guy."

He lay with closed eyes, listening to her light footsteps as she went from the room.

No one in that house, striving after the oblivion and the release from thought that lay in sleep, remembered the lamp Doe had left burning on the table.

A lamp, quite forgotten by three distress-harried people— burning clearly, sending through the window just beyond it a glow that could be seen for a long way.

CHAPTER XVIII

ANOTHER MURDER

On the night that Finley and his son were killed, while word was carried to the scattered hill dwellers calling them to join in the hunt for a man who had made himself by those brutal murders an outcast whose life must be forfeit to the law, Gage Hardin rode onward into the fastnesses of the forests.

The next morning at daylight, Shamus Harrigan was cooking his breakfast in the kitchen back of his store. Harrigan's store was about the last outpost that the lonely mountain frontier knew. Finishing his breakfast, Harrigan walked softly from the living rooms back of the store into the store itself, to prepare for the day.

The date was the first of the month. The day was Saturday. Date and day were a profitable conjunction for Harrigan. Since there was no other place to meet for sociable intercourse and pastime, men from the isolated ranches beyond the store gathered there to play cards, to jest with Harrigan, and to enjoy the society of Harrigan's lovely daughter Eileen.

Harrigan walked on tiptoe out of the living rooms because Eileen was, he thought, still asleep. He erred. Eileen had wakened, she heard him going into the store, and she slipped out of bed and began to dress.

Harrigan stopped at the end of the store, before his old-fashioned safe, took from the safe a container of money, and closed the safe door. He placed the money container on the counter and began counting out the change for the day's business.

The outer door swung inward, and Harrigan raised his head at the sound. He had unlocked the door scarcely a half hour before. He saw a big man confronting him, a man with black eyes, with black spade beard covering the lower part of his face. The man was covering Harrigan with a drawn gun.

"I need food," the man announced. "Don't get excited, and you won't get hurt."

But Shamus Harrigan was one of those excitable men who lose their heads easily. He glanced down at the money container on the counter. Would the man demand food only, with that money lying in plain sight? Shamus had never been held up before. He stood in stark immobility.

The big man spoke again, his voice roughened by impatience. "Hurry, will you? I haven't all day to wait. I don't want to shoot, but I will if you don't move fast enough."

Harrigan's lips quivered in pure fright. His one coherent thought was to hide the money in some fashion, as he went to procure the demanded food, without rendering the act of doing so conspicuous. He started to sidle away, then swayed back toward the counter. His hand darted toward the money container. The man beyond the counter fired.

The report of the revolver was deafening in the small room. The man's voice cut through the reverberations.

Shamus could not hear. There was a roaring din in his ears. He knew he was hurt. He had felt the bullet strike. His head seemed suddenly enormously heavy and light at the same time. He sagged to the floor, but he could still remember the money lying there on the counter. Eileen would hear the shot. She would come, in time to save the money.

She did hear the shot, not being deaf. She came running into the room just in time to see a large man darting out of the store. The money container was still on the counter. She had never seen death before, but she knew that Shamus Harrigan was dead. Too stunned to think, acting solely on instinct, the girl ran after the fleeing man, and reached the narrow porch across the front of the store just in time to see the fugitive fling himself on his gray horse and race out of sight into the trees lining the road.

She started to go back into the store, then her eyes dilated as she remembered what she had seen there on the floor. She stopped short. A scream stopped in her throat, as she flung up one hand to press against her paling lips. Then her terror conquered. The scream broke through.

From the opposite direction to that which the killer had taken, another man rode madly into the roadway, reined in his horse before her, and leaped from the horse's back to the porch platform. He reached out both hands to grip her arms in a steadying pressure, and she stared at him insanely.

"What happened?" he demanded. "I heard a shot. Oh, am I too late again? Has any one been hurt?"

"My—my father!" Eileen gasped, and wavered on her feet.

The man who gripped her arms stilled. "He's not dead!"

Eileen fought with her panic-roughened breath. "Yes. He—he's dead."

"You saw the man who killed him?"

"Only a glimpse."

"What was he like?"

"He——" Eileen raised her eyes. For the first time she really saw the man who stood before her. "He—black beard —black eyes, he—he had a gray horse."

"I expected that. There was nothing else you could tell me?"

The girl slowly shook her head. "Nothing. Only, he had no hat."

"Listen." The man held her gaze, shaking her slightly to force her entire attention. "You stay right here. I'm going inside for a moment. Don't move. I'll be back immediately."

He released her arms from his grip and strode into the store. One glance at Harrigan told him all he needed to know in that quarter. But—beyond Harrigan, lying on the very edge of the counter, as if it might have been caught there, dislodged from a man's head, a man who dared take no time to recover it, lay a hat. It was a black, wide-brimmed Stetson hat.

Eileen started to attention, as the man emerged from the store, carrying a black hat in his hand. He said:

"The reason he had no hat when you saw him was that he dropped it somehow in the store, and had no time to pick it up. I found it on the edge of the counter."

He held the black hat out for her inspection, upside down. Embroidered into the leather sweatband, sweat-stained blue thread against sweat-stained tan leather, was the name, "Gage Hardin." Mary Silver had sewed those letters there. The man who stood staring down at the hat gripped in his fingers wondered what woman's hand had made identification of that hat so indisputable. He did not voice the thought.

"Did he take the money?" Eileen, too, was staring down at the black hat. "Dad had it on the counter, counting out the day's change. He always did that. In the divided compartment out of the cash drawer. Dad always took it out of the drawer at night and put it in the safe." She set her teeth on a choking sob. "Checks in one compartment, ten-dollar bills next to the checks, then the fives—oh, you know!"

Apparently the money was untouched, the man returned shortly to report, save that the five-dollar and ten-dollar bills were gone.

"Are you here alone?" he asked. "Where's your mother?"

"Oh—mother!" The girl fought for balance and coherency. "How will I tell her?" Momentarily beyond further speech, Eileen broke into unrestrained sobbing.

The man stepped close to her and laid one arm across her shoulders.

"You needn't. I'll tell her, if you'll only say where I can

find her. Can you try to listen to me, miss? My name is Weaver, Chuck Weaver. I'll do anything I can, if you can manage to brace up and tell me what you want done."

"I want to go to mother." Eileen relaxed against his sustaining arm. "She's up the trail about five miles, at the Redding ranch. She went there last night. Mrs. Redding was sick, and they came for mother. There's no real road, just a trail through the woods."

"A trail's enough," the man interrupted. "Come get on my horse. I'll take you to your mother."

"But we can't—leave him—lying in there alone, that way."

"There's nothing else to do," said Weaver gently. "No one will bother him. I'll lock the door and take the key with me. Come."

In the small cleared space before the rough, unpainted Redding house, he stopped his horse and lifted the girl to the ground. As easily and carefully as if she had been a tired child, he carried her up the three low steps to the porch and placed her on a homemade bench sitting against the wall to the right of the door. He had left the black hat tied behind his saddle.

His cautious rap brought response from within almost immediately. He removed his own headgear as the door swung open to reveal a stout, dark woman with a tired face.

"May I see Mrs. Harrigan, please?" Weaver requested quietly.

"I'm Mrs. Harrigan. What is it?"

"Will you try to be prepared for a shock, Mrs. Harrigan? Your husband has been killed by a holdup man. I'm sorry."

Mrs. Harrigan's dark face contorted, smoothed. She opened her mouth, closed it, and held herself rigidly upright. "That was probably the best way. I'm used to facing harsh things without preparation. You're—a stranger. You——"

"I am Chuck Weaver, lady. Your daughter is here. I brought her——"

"Eileen! Oh! I—I——"

"I know. Right here on the bench. Will you send any man around——"

"There's only Mr. Redding and the hired man, Coates. They——"

"Will you send them down to the store, please? And—Mrs. Harrigan"—Weaver laid a hand on her shoulder—"there are things to be done. You can leave it all to me, if you will."

"Th-thank you." She stepped past him. "Eileen!"

Weaver turned away. Her voice followed him.

"I'm not being very grateful. I—I can't say any more, now. I'm leaving to you the—things to be done."

Weaver looked up from the bottom step. "Yes. You *can* leave them to me. I'm only sorry I can't do more." And he was gone then on the black horse that waited him; muttering to himself that which no other ear could hear save his own: "Well, he'll not get that far ahead of me again. He'll kill no more storekeepers."

CHAPTER XIX

RIDERS IN THE NIGHT

SWEDE THOBURN went to sleep within two minutes after his head touched the pillow on Doe Gaston's bed, but Doe lay awake, restless, wondering whether or not the morning ever would come. The sleep he strove to woo eluded him persistently, so that he was lying taut, almost painfully aware of every least sound in the night, when there became faintly audible the rhythm of horse's hoofs approaching over the sun-hardened ground.

Doe raised himself on one elbow, the better to listen. Every instant brought the sound nearer. Doe slipped out of bed, cautiously, in order not to awaken Thoburn. His caution was superfluous, had he known it—nothing short of an earthquake could have wakened Swede Thoburn.

Doe moved silently into the next room, the room where Shawnessy lay, closing the door behind him.

"I heard it," said Shawnessy from his bed. "Who now? It couldn't be Baker this soon."

"Impossible," answered Doe, and saw with a start of surprise that he had forgotten to put out the lamp on the table. "Long has barely had time to reach the J Bar B. Well, the horse has stopped in the yard. I might as well open the door."

He crossed the room and suited the action to the word, just as a man ascended the back porch steps.

"Howdy," Doe greeted dryly. "Come in."

Into the room stepped an elderly man with a clipped gray beard, with sharp gray eyes under jutting brows.

"Howdy," he turned. "Sorry to be intruding at this hour of the night, but I have to find my destination as quickly as

I can. I got as far as the ridge above the valley. I was going to turn north, but I saw your light burning and headed for it. I am looking for the Circle Crossbar and Gage Hardin. Can you direct me?"

"You're there," said Doe. "But Gage isn't home."

"I know that. Are you Doe Gaston?"

"I am."

"I thought you must be. I'm Shark Hoaley, from the Flying MH Joined, down on the desert. You may have heard Hardin speak of me."

"I certainly have!" Doe reached for a chair and proffered it to the older man. "Sit down, Mr. Hoaley. This is the sheriff, Guy Shawnessy. He—hasn't been well, had to remain here for a while. What did you want to see Gage about? Anything I can do?"

Hoaley fixed him with an intent scrutiny.

"You know why I've come, don't you, Gaston? Some wild report came in by passing rider, of a man named Gage Hardin, who was going about here in the backwoods murdering isolated storekeepers. That report doesn't sound like the Gage Hardin I met—and I remembered very clearly what he told me about the trouble-making faction in Great Lost Valley. I dug up my old gun and came. What's going on up here, anyway?"

Shawnessy sat up in bed and reached for his clothes.

"It's all hearsay. If what we've been told is true, Gage has held up two stores and killed two people. We received word of the killings only tonight. The man who brought it is in the next room asleep. I'm leaving here at daybreak with a posse."

"Well, it's lucky that you had a light burning!" Hoaley returned. "If it hadn't been for that lamp, I'd have gone on up the valley, instead of coming here to ask for direction. You'd probably have been gone before I'd learned that I was going in the wrong direction and turned back here."

"There isn't any doubt about it," said Doe Gaston. "Likely I'll always be glad I forgot to blow out that lamp."

"You're going with the posse?" Shawnessy drew on his trousers, stepping to the floor.

"That's what I came for, sheriff. I'll have to ask you for a mountain-bred horse. Old Scotch isn't so good in the hills."

"You can have two of 'em," Shawnessy answered. "We have to——" He paused, in the act of cinching his belt, as sound again broke the night, sound of a horse's hoofs, hoofs of a horse ridden hard. Shawnessy glanced at Gaston with raised brows. "This is getting to be a habit, Doe. Who now, do you reckon?"

"The Circle Crossbar is getting popular," said Doe dryly.

The three listened in silence, as the running horse turned down the lane, into the yard, and plunged to a halt. The thud of running feet crossed the yard, and Doe leaped up to step to the door and swing it wide. An exhausted man staggered into the room. He stared from one to another of the three men he faced.

"Can you direct me to the Circle Crossbar, boys? I saw your light and——"

"This is the Circle Crossbar." Doe shoved a chair under him, as he swayed on his feet. "Things are happening too fast. What is it now?"

The man almost fell into the seat, with a thankful upward glance at Gaston.

"Sorry. I've been riding like a fool to get here. The telegraph lines are still down. Changed horses three times. Haven't slept since I started. I—which of you is the sheriff?"

Doe pointed, and the man's gaze centered on Shawnessy.

"We need you back in the mountains, sheriff. Fellow shot up, named Harrigan. Swell guy. Awful thing. The killer lost his hat. I brought it."

He jerked a tightly rolled bundle from his pocket and tossed it on the bed behind the erect Shawnessy. The bundle was a crumpled black hat. Shawnessy turned and bent his head, and knew without picking it up whose hat it was. It had lighted on its flattened, crushed crown, wrong side up. He could see the dingy letters shouting at him from the sweatband—"Gage Hardin." No one spoke.

All three men were staring at the hat, stupidly, as if they had never seen a hat before. They were too completely engrossed by their stupefaction to be aware that Mary Silver had come into the room—till they heard her cry, and knew by that cry that she had already encompassed the entire situation, had seen the hat lying there on the bed. And they knew that because she cried out only a name.

"Oh, Gage! *Gage!*"

Shawnessy's cold gaze darted to Doc Gaston. His face had gone white. "You two get out of here, Doc, and leave me alone with Mary. There can no longer be any doubt. Two? I must be getting loco myself. All three of you get out. You and Hoaley, Doc, take this man outside and get all he has to tell. Go quickly, will you?"

Before he had ceased speaking, the three men were on their feet and moving toward the door that led to the porch, faces averted from Mary's stricken gaze. She stood quite still as the door closed behind them, then she swayed on her feet, and Shawnessy leaped toward her to catch her as she fainted in his arms. He carried her to a chair and laid her gently down.

He went to a bench standing against a wall by the outer door, wet his handkerchief in the pail of water standing there, and came back to lave her face with the dripping linen. He wondered if her pain could be worse than his, since his pain was two-edged, both for her and Gage Hardin. She opened her eyes and looked up at him.

"Guy!" She caught his hand in a tight grip. "It isn't true. It can't be true."

She was sobbing, uncontrollable sobs that shook her. Then

suddenly her arms went around his neck, but she was beyond speech. Shawnessy laid his face against her hair.

Her sobs abated to long, hard breaths. "Guy! You're so—decent. Why couldn't I have loved you in the first place?"

"Don't ask me such a thing!" Shawnessy's mouth was rimmed with a thin white line. "I've asked Fate that, a thousand times."

CHAPTER XX

IN the dark hours of the silent night, Shawnessy rode doggedly to reach a man in Dead Spring, a small town twenty miles away. The man in Dead Spring owned a small hand press. He had done printing jobs for the sheriff before. Shawnessy talked to him rapidly and crisply for a few minutes. The printer voiced a loud protest.

"Gosh, sheriff! That will take me two hours!"

"Sorry," snapped Shawnessy. "I can't help it. Get them out. If it takes you all night, get them out. Get them out on the stage that leaves at six o'clock. Get them all over the county, and don't waste time doing it."

Daylight was breaking as Shawnessy rode into the yard at the Circle Crossbar.

The printer in Dead Spring was working at feverish speed, grumbling to himself as he worked. "Well, that's the craziest dodger I ever printed. But if Shawnessy says so, I suppose it goes. I wonder what he meant by that last paragraph? Probably none of my business. He's ordered it, and it has to go."

It went. By stage, by rider, by every means at command, it was being sent far and wide all through the county as the sun came up over the hills. It went into store windows. It went into the forest and found resting place on the boles of trees. It flared from telegraph poles along the few main-traveled roads.

It gleamed whitely in a spot deep in the woods north of Harrigan's store on the bark of a white pine. Before the pine a rider halted his horse to read the dodger. He smoothed his black spade beard with an idle hand. On his black hair he wore a light-tan hat. The hat was very new,

119

the fact was apparent at the merest glance. The man leaned forward in his saddle to study the dodger closely, and an enigmatic smile twisted his mouth as he read:

WANTED

Gage Hardin, for murder and robbery.

$10,000 reward.

Height, 6 feet 3 inches. Weight, 210 pounds. Hair and eyes black. Black spade beard and black mustache. When last seen was wearing dark blue flannel shirt, black batwing chaps, dark gray pants, black boots, red-and-blue neckerchief, and black hat. He was riding a gray horse.

IMPORTANT!

This man must be brought in alive. No part of the reward will be paid to anyone who brings him in dead or seriously wounded. Anyone finding trace of this man notify Guy Shawnessy, sheriff of Grant County.

The big man in the light-tan hat sat immobile in his saddle, and his gaze was focused with singular intensity on that final paragraph. His absorption was rudely disturbed at sound of movement in the brush and trees at his right. He turned his head, frowning, gazing at the area from which the sound had come.

A man rode out of the brush in that place to emerge into the small clearing surrounding the white pine tree. He could not have come from any trail or road, since there was no trail or road within miles. He was small and lean, with a long, dour face. A brush of unshaved sandy stubble littered his jaws, streaked with gray. He rode a gaunt, fleabitten roan. He drew the roan to a stop, surveying the man who had been studying the dodger.

"Are you Gage Hardin?"

"I am." Hardin smiled. "What can I do for you?"

"You can't do anything for me. I've come to do something for you. I've brought you something." From the side pocket of his leather jacket he took a folded piece of wrapping paper—the paper had come from Harrigan's store. He extended the fold toward Hardin. "It's supposed to be all-fired important, to some people."

Hardin accepted the folded paper, turned it over in his fingers, and lifted his glance to the man on the fleabitten roan.

"What is it?"

"Open it and read it," the small man answered curtly. "Then you'll know as much as I do."

Hardin unfolded the slip of paper, conscious of a feeling of vast curiosity. On the wrapping paper, in a clear, legible hand, was written:

HARDIN: You will have seen the dodgers. You won't know me, but my name is Chuck Weaver. The man who brings you this note is Billy Pitchell. He is nobody's friend and nobody's enemy; he is loyal, and you can trust him.

I know that you held up Casper Loody's store at Elks Crossing. I know that Everett Finley's store was next held up—Finley and his son Rusty were killed. Finley died describing a man who would seem to be you, and naming the man as Gage Hardin. I know that Harrigan's store was held up the next morning and Harrigan was foully murdered. The man who committed the murder left on the counter a black hat with the name, "Gage Hardin," stitched into the sweatband.

I want you to give your answer to Pitchell. He will bring it to me. You needn't write it. He'll remember.

There has been a fight among Peele's men. One man whom Peele called Oaks went wild and killed two of the others before he was downed. Louis Peele is one short day's ride ahead of you in a little blind gully leading off the head of Lave Rock Canyon, to the left as you go in.

Where did you lose that hat?

CHUCK WEAVER.

Hardin studied the note for a full minute after he had read it, then lifted his gaze again to the small man on the fleabitten roan. He scrutinized the man's features from hairline to chin. That was a useless procedure. Nothing was to be read on that leathery countenance or in the pale flint-hard eyes which adorned it.

"Who in time is Chuck Weaver?"

Pitchell grinned without mirth. "He told me you'd say that. He always calls the turn. He's Chuck Weaver, that's all. I can't tell you anything about him, only he's no man to fool with. And he has a funny com—comp—yes, that's it, that's what he said, a funny complex. He said to me: 'Billy, I have a funny complex. I can't bear to see the innocent suffer. I must know whether or not Hardin did any of this killing.' You see, I read the note."

Hardin smiled wryly. "Well, Pitchell, I know no Chuck Weaver. Does he know me?"

Pitchell shook his head with a great deal of emphasis. "Just knows who you are, that's all. He saw you once. As far as he knows, you might have done the killing, but he doesn't believe it. He has to admit that things look bad for you, so bad that they have him guessing. But he can't bear to see the innocent suffer. He's funny that way. Yet if that's being funny—why, I'll take mine funny. He's a man, even if he is bad—or maybe has been bad."

"Does he know Louis Peele?" Hardin asked, wondering whether or not any key lay there concerning this man who called himself Chuck Weaver, who had unceremoniously thrust himself into his, Hardin's, complicated affairs without so much as a by-your-leave.

Whatever reaction Hardin had hoped to get to that query, none was forthcoming. Pitchell answered as casually as if Hardin had asked him the time of day.

"Yes, sure. Knows him well. Peele was a pal of his, years ago. He told me that himself. He's following Peele right now, waiting a chance to get Peele away from his gang and talk to him alone. I told you he was funny—Chuck, I mean. He doesn't trust anybody. He doesn't want any one in that gang to see him but Louis Peele. I'd make a guess that he has a good reason for not wanting any one to get a look at him."

"You're strangely willing to tell anything you know about this Chuck Weaver and his affairs, aren't you?" Hardin's eyes bored him through.

"Why shouldn't I be?" Pitchell shrugged his lack of all responsibility in the matter. "I haven't anything to do with it. I'm simply obeying Chuck's orders. He directed me to answer any questions you might ask, and not to do any lying. Well, you've been asking questions, haven't you?"

Hardin took refuge in silence, and again he gazed at the curious note in his hand. He refolded it slowly.

"You can return this letter to Chuck Weaver. I think I can guess what he is to Louis Peele, and just about how long ago Peele was a pal of his. You can tell him that for me. Did he ever say anything to you about seventy-five one-thousand-dollar bills, Pitchell?"

"Seventy-five thousand!" For the first time Pitchell betrayed real emotion to Hardin's observant gaze. He gaped and stared. "Good gosh, no!"

Hardin's smile was not wry now, it was significant and almost sneering.

"Well, you can tell him also, for me, that I don't know any more about that money than he does, if that's what is bothering him. As to all this killing that's been going on, and my guilt in the matter, tell him that I sent this reply to his wondering: 'What do *you* think?' Also, you can tell him he'll never get to Louis Peele if I can get to Peele first. And, lastly, you can tell him that I didn't *lose* that hat. Somebody carried it off one night while I lay asleep in a canyon."

"By glory!" crowed Pitchell. "He said that was what happened. He said he'd bet his last dollar on it."

"Oh, did he? Well, can you remember what I've told you to say to him?"

"I can remember anything." Pitchell turned his fleabitten roan about, and without another word rode into the brush, in the direction from which he had come.

Hardin sat his saddle, gazing intently at the trees but seeing nothing, whispering to himself:

"So, a fellow whom Peele called Oaks went wild, did he? It couldn't have been anybody but Tamm. I don't get this. There were four men lying back there under that rock heap where Guy overtook Peele and his men. The one on top was Red Corcoran. I shouldn't be such an all-fired fool. I should have looked at the rest of them, and not taken it for granted that they must be the remaining three of the Four from Hell's Hill.

"I wonder if Dutch and Salt River Charley can be alive still, held prisoners by Peele? It wasn't like Tamm to go off his head and raise a fuss, knowing only too well that he'd get killed for it. I wish that this mysterious Chuck Weaver had been a little more plain. And I wish I knew just who Chuck Weaver is."

As he turned away from the white pine on the bark of which the dodger was posted, his thoughts ran swiftly ahead of him. It had been a wild shot, that, asking Pitchell whether or not Chuck Weaver had ever mentioned the seventy-five thousand dollars taken from the pack train.

"No," Hardin told himself impatiently, "it didn't strike fire because it was so damn impossible. That fellow couldn't be Creegan. No man could have gotten out of that swamp alive. So I can't place Chuck Weaver, I guess. I can't even place what he is—not exactly a friend, and not entirely an enemy. Sitting on the fence, that's what. A man sitting on the fence can see both sides, and use them to his own ends. Well, this is an unequal game, Mr. Weaver, but we'll play it out to the last card—" And his gaze clung to the dodger as he rode away.

CHAPTER XXI

SMOKING TRAIL

THAT morning on which Guy Shawnessy ordered the dodgers made, he ate an early, hurried breakfast with Doe Gaston, Shark Hoaley, Swede Thoburn, and Mary Silver. Kipps Tanner, the man who had brought the report of Harrigan's murder, was still asleep. He had requested to be allowed to sleep until the last moment, declaring fervently that he needed sleep far more than he needed food. Jeff Baker had arrived a half hour before Shawnessy's return, and was out in the barn helping to saddle and bridle mounts for the entire group.

Shawnessy was the first to arise from the table, having eaten hastily, impatient with every added delay. The other men rose to join him, and he turned to Doe Gaston with a brief request.

"Take the men on out to the barn, Doe. I want a last word with Mary."

Without verbal response, Doe led Swede and Hoaley out of the room and across the yard. Mary still sat at the table, her food untouched, engrossed with thoughts that she shrank from making articulate.

"Mary." Shawnessy closed the door behind Doe and leaned against it. "Come here."

The girl rose from the table, went to him, and stood before him, her haggard eyes raised to his stern, blond face.

"Yes, Guy?"

He placed one arm about her and drew her to him, smiling down into her face. From his pocket he drew a sheet of paper and held it up for her to read. It was his holographic draft of the dodger. Her eyes followed every sentence with

125

avid interest, and slowed to read again that significant final paragraph.

"I told you I would protect him from injury." Shawnessy's gaze also was on those terse words:

This man must be brought in alive. No part of the reward will be paid to anyone who brings him in dead or seriously wounded.

"Nothing more is needed," Shawnessy added. "Anybody making an effort to capture him will let him get away, after reading that, rather than risk the chance of injuring him. I'll take him alive and unhurt. And if——"

"And if you find that he *did* do it," interrupted Mary Silver, "no matter what drove him to it, it will have to be the end of everything between him and me. But if he did *not* do it, bring him back to me."

"It was needless to ask that. What else could I do?" Shawnessy's clear eyes lingered on her face. "If I come back to you alone, you will know that bringing him to you was beyond my power, or beyond my jurisdiction. I don't believe there is anything more to be said between you and me—at least, not now."

"There is this," said Mary. "That if you do come back alone, there will be waiting for you whatever I can give to further your happiness."

There was nothing in Shawnessy's face to betray the emotion that surged within him at the clear inference of her words. He reached one hand behind him and opened the door.

"And if I bring him to you, maybe now and then you will both have a little time for me. There are many kinds of happiness, Mary."

He went out and closed the door behind him. She returned slowly to the chair in which she had been sitting by the table. From that position the men outside were beyond her range of vision through the window. She heard the sound of low-voiced admonition and brief interchange of comment, the unrhythmic clatter of horses' hoofs departing.

Two days later Shawnessy rode into Elks Crossing at the head of his posse, dismounted, and preceded his men into Casper Loody's store. Loody's greeting gaze dropped from Shawnessy's face to the badge of authority he wore, and lifted again to meet Shawnessy's eyes.

"I came as quickly as I could." Shawnessy gestured to the side wall of the store. "I see you have the dodger posted."

"Yes. They came in on the stage this morning. Well, I'll just tell you exactly what happened when Hardin came in here. I was——"

"Just a minute," Shawnessy interrupted. "Suppose you let me ask questions and you do the answering. And whatever you do, don't exaggerate, and don't let your imagination run away with you. Did this man answer to the description on the dodgers?"

"In every way. Even to the gray horse. I could see the horse clearly in the light shining from the store window. I noticed that the bridle and the saddle on the horse were silver-mounted, and I could have sworn they were made of gray leather."

Shawnessy glanced at Baker. "Well, that was Hardin all right. There can't be any doubt of it." He turned his attention back to Loody. "Can you say truthfully that he held you up? Did he flash a gun on you?"

Loody hesitated. "We-we-ell, I'd call it holding somebody up. He was wearing two guns——"

"Did he *draw* either of them?" Shawnessy demanded sharply. "Be careful about allowing any feeling of injury to distort your statements as to what really happened, Loody."

"Yes, sir. No, he didn't draw any gun." Loody subsided,

sufficiently intimidated by Shawnessy's brusque command to strive for accuracy rather than the exhibition of his own importance. "He just walked in here and asked for food. He didn't try to get tough with me, even explained what he was here for, and said he'd pay for the food later. I got him what he asked for, and told him he didn't owe me anything if what he'd said was the truth. Then he went out and rode away. That's about all there was to it."

Shawnessy gave a short laugh. "Well, so far we seem to have been making a lot of fuss about nothing. We'd better be getting on to Finley's where something did happen. One last question, Loody. What of the fellow who told you where to find me?"

"I'd say he was every bit as big as Hardin, sheriff. He would almost answer the same description. Only he was riding a black horse. He just stepped in here, advised me to send for you, and then got out, like he was in a hurry, or didn't want me to get too good a look at him."

"Thanks." Shawnessy turned toward the door. "There's nothing more to be learned here, Jeff. Let's get moving."

As the posse remounted, Shark Hoaley addressed Shawnessy.

"Has Hardin made a habit of wearing a beard, sheriff?"

Shawnessy smiled. "I wouldn't call it habit, Hoaley. But I've seen him several times when he *was* wearing one, simply because, as in the present instance, keeping his face cleanly shaven was temporarily inconvenient. His beard grows naturally spade-shaped. I wish it might be possible that investigation at the Finley and the Harrigan stores could simmer down to as innocent an affair as this did at Loody's."

Finley's store was closed when the posse reached it, and Swede Thoburn led the way to the Finley house. The other men remained sitting their horses, while Shawnessy went up to the house and rapped on the door. Finley's widow answered his knock—a thin little thing with a tired, lined face.

She glanced up at his height, at the badge on his breast, and made an indefinite gesture of welcome.

"Come in, sheriff. It seems like you've been awfully long in getting here. I was——"

"I haven't time to come in, Mrs. Finley. I only want to ask you a few questions. Did you see the robber the night the store was held up?"

Mrs. Finley's answer was prompt and unequivocal. "No, sir. I wasn't at the store that night. I was here at home when it happened. Swede Thoburn is the only person who can really know anything. And I suppose you've talked with Swede."

"Yes, I sure have." Shawnessy hesitated, studying her. "And very likely you can't tell us anything about this man who sent Swede after me, either?"

Mrs. Finley's lined face brightened. "Oh, yes, I can. I saw him. He came down here to the house after Swede left. He was a rough-looking man, but he was awfully nice to me. He—well, he gave me some money."

Shawnessy could not quite control a slight start. "He gave you *money?*"

"Yes. He said he knew that I would be subjected to a lot of unexpected expense, the kind of expense people were never prepared for. He said he knew it would make things a little less awful if I didn't have to worry about money, along with everything else."

"Had you ever seen this man before?" queried Shawnessy, watching her face for the least betraying expression. "Was he anything to you or to any member of your family, that he should give you money?"

The sincerity in the woman's thin face was not to be doubted. She answered vehemently and without hesitation.

"No, sir! I had never seen him before. I guess the only explanation is that he did it out of kindness of heart. I was so dumfounded I barely managed to thank him before he was gone. He just shoved the money into my hand, and went, and I didn't know till after I came back into the house that what he had given me was two one-thousand-dollar bills."

"Two one-thousand-dollar bills!" Shawnessy echoed. For a moment he remained silent, in a startled study, his thoughts gone racing down pathways of which the woman could not dream. In the next instant he shook himself out of his shock. "May I see the bills, please? It is very possible that they might play an important part in solving this case, Mrs. Finley."

"Why, of course. Just wait a moment until I get them."

When she brought them to him, he turned them over in his hands, giving them a close and minute scrutiny. They were old, thumbed, and worn, but they were good legal currency. He took a pencil and notebook from his pocket, jotted down the serial numbers of the bills, and returned them to the waiting woman.

"You'd better put those bills in the bank, as quickly as possible, Mrs. Finley." He returned his notebook to his pocket. "Thank you for your courtesy. I have an idea that you will have proved a great deal of help to me. Adios, Mrs. Finley."

He joined the waiting men, remounted his horse, and led the way down the road for several rods before he spoke. And he spoke then only in answer to the question asked by Jeff Baker, who could hold his tongue and his curiosity no longer. Baker asked if he had learned anything.

"Yes, I certainly did, Jeff." Shawnessy turned in the saddle to center his attention collectively on the entire group. "But you won't realize the significance of it till I explain something else to you."

With as much brevity as he could use and still encompass the situation, he gave them a detailed account of the robbery of the pack train which had occurred near Hell's Hill years before, with its loot of seventy-five one-thousand-dollar bills. He finished by disclosing the amazing gift Chuck Weaver had made Mrs. Finley.

"There's something radically unreasonable in the facts we have uncovered here," he added. "Men riding the hills in secret, carefully keeping themselves clear of intercourse with their fellow men, do not commonly go about carrying thousand-dollar bills in their pockets. Nor do they make a practice of bestowing such gifts on bereft widows they have never seen before."

"I'd say there was something mighty odd about this Chuck Weaver hombre," Baker said tersely. "He makes himself pretty scarce most of the time, then he deliberately comes out into the open at the scene of a murder for no particular reason and broadcasts his identity."

"But—*does* he?" Shawnessy countered, and his meaning was unmistakable. "You don't believe that Chuck Weaver is his right name, do you? Not for a minute, Jeff. I'll lay you a bet right now that when we finally run him down we'll find that his real name is Sidney, Bluex, or Creegan."

Old Shark Hoaley whistled. "We're striking a warm trail, Shawnessy."

Shawnessy laughed. "Warm? It's getting so hot it smokes!"

The evening dusk was falling when the posse halted and dismounted before Harrigan's store. The sheriff walked in to find Mrs. Harrigan alone, behind the counter. Her relief at his arrival was instantaneous and voluble, but when he asked to see her daughter, she spread her hands in apologetic deprecation.

"She's not here, sheriff. I sent her to my sister, more than twenty-five miles from here, so she could get it out of her mind like. She couldn't bear to talk to you even if she was here. It was an awful thing for her to have seen. Mr. Redding has been taking care of the store for me. I only happen to be here now because I'm tending store so he could go home to his supper. But I know everything that Eileen had to tell. Redding's man brought you the hat the robber left, didn't he?"

"Yes, I have the hat," the sheriff assured her. "I understand, from what Redding's man told me, that this Chuck Weaver appeared from nowhere, brought Eileen to you at the Redding ranch, came back to the store and took care of Mr. Harrigan, then returned to the Redding ranch, bringing you the store keys, sent Redding himself for the nearest neighbor, and sent Redding's man for me, giving him the hat to deliver to me. Is that correct?"

"Yes, that's exactly what happened." A frown of uneasiness crossed Mrs. Harrigan's broad face. "But why are you asking so much about Chuck Weaver? He hasn't done anything."

"He seems to have done a great deal," Shawnessy replied. "Had you ever seen him before? Was he anything to you or to any member of your family?"

"He was not. None of us had ever seen him before. The way I take it, he was just a kind-hearted stranger who chanced to be passing by."

"He seems to have a genius for chancing to pass by where things are happening," the sheriff replied grimly. "You realize, don't you, Mrs. Harrigan, that anything which occurred might prove of the utmost importance? Are you sure you are not withholding anything about this Chuck Weaver?"

Mrs. Harrigan started and her eyes widened. She had been taken off guard, and because she was a woman not given to evasion, her tongue moved with the instinct to give honest answer. "Why, yes. He—he gave me——" She caught the stammering words and forced herself to silence.

"He gave you two one-thousand-dollar bills," Shawnessy supplied quietly.

"No, he gave me three." Mrs. Harrigan capitulated, but patently under inner protest. "I didn't want anybody to know about that. I hid the money. I haven't had a chance to bank it yet. I can't understand how *you* found it out. I hadn't told a soul."

"It doesn't matter," the sheriff hastened to reassure her. "Don't be alarmed. There's nothing incriminating in your having the money. But those bills may prove to be very important, and I'd like to see them and get their serial numbers. Do you have them here?"

"Yes, I have. I have them right where they've been ever since he gave them to me. I'll just go in the back room and get them."

Presently she returned and handed the three bills to the sheriff. She stood waiting anxiously while he copied the necessary information from the currency, and heaved a sigh of relief when the money was again in her possession.

"A man usually carries bills in a wallet, or folder of some sort, Mrs. Harrigan. Did you get a chance to see whether Weaver took those bills you have there from a well-filled wallet, or perhaps from a sizable roll?"

"He had them in a worn old wallet," Mrs. Harrigan answered readily. "And they were all he had. He told me so, when he gave them to me. He said that was the last of his ready cash, and he hoped he wouldn't have any more bills to settle. I didn't know what he meant. I shouldn't think a man with all that money in his pocket would be going around running up bills."

"Bills to settle," mused the sheriff. "I have an idea that he didn't mean the kind of bills you think he did, Mrs. Harrigan. Mm-m-m. That seems to be about all of that. Now, about the robber himself. Of course, I have Eileen's report, from Redding's man, but I'd like you to confirm it. He was a big man, black hair and eyes, square black beard, he was riding a gray horse. Is that correct?"

"Yes. That was about all she had time to see."

"And he took from the compartment out of the cash drawer only the five-dollar and ten-dollar bills?"

"That's right, sheriff."

"Do you know about how much money he got?" pursued Shawnessy.

"I know exactly how much he got!" Mrs. Harrigan was very positive about that. "There was a little over six hundred dollars, six hundred and twenty, in ten-dollar bills, and three hundred and forty-five dollars in five-dollar bills."

Shawnessy studied that over for a moment. "I don't suppose there'd be any way in which you could possibly identify any one of those bills, would there? Ordinary currency is pretty hard to identify positively."

Mrs. Harrigan brightened. "Well, yes, that's right. But there's one of those bills I'd know again, one of the ten-dollar bills. Recently we received a circular about some counterfeit ten-dollar bills. And it warned everybody who got a brand-new ten-dollar bill not to pass it out to anybody else, but to turn it in to a bank. Last week, Lige Neumann, who has a little place about five miles from here, came in to get some groceries, and he had a brand-new ten-dollar bill. I know Lige is all right, but I asked him where *he* got it, and told him why I wanted to know.

"He'd been in the city, a few days before that, and he'd got it at Meyers Department Store. So I just wrote along the edge of the bill, 'Lige Neumann, Meyers,' and we were keeping it there for Mr. Harrigan to take to the bank next time he went in. All the rest of it was just money. But I'd know *that* bill again."

"Yes, Mrs. Harrigan, and so would I!" returned Shawnessy. "Well, I'll say so long, and—thank you. We must be moving on."

CHAPTER XXII

SALT RIVER'S REVOLT

THAT day was the one on which Gage Hardin sat his horse scrutinizing the dodger on the bole of the white pine, where Billy Pitchell brought him the note from Weaver, a good many miles north of Harrigan's store. It was the day and hour in which Louis Peele and his men, in the little blind gully leading off the head of Lava Rock Canyon, were arguing among themselves with a heat that was dangerously liable to culminate in disastrous combustion.

"I'm getting goddam sick of skulking ahead of Gage Hardin!" Weeny Hatteras expressed his resentment, with a pugnacity that evidenced a reckless disregard of the consequences that might attend such an assertion. "How long are we going to be forced to lie around here in the woods like this, because of some cockeyed idea you're nursing about getting your hands on that money?"

"Shut up!" The light in Peele's eyes was flagrant warning. "*I'm* getting sick of hearing you harp on the subject of that money. I know what I'm doing. I know a good many things you don't know. We've almost got Hardin where we want him. The sheriff is after him right now. That killing at the Harrigan store would send Guy Shawnessy even after his best friend."

"It's funny the sheriff tacked on that sentence about taking him alive." Dick France glowered at Peele from under frowning brows. "What was his idea? That's what I'd like to know."

"What do you care?" Peele retorted. "It plays into our hands, doesn't it? All he has to do now is to stick Hardin in jail. Then we can get busy. You want to remember that all

135

this fuss that's been kicked up about Hardin has drawn Shawnessy's attention off us."

Salt River Charley edged abruptly into the conversation, an obscure expression flickering in his eyes, too veiled for Peele to read. "To go back to an old question, Louis, how are you so sure that Hardin knows where that money is?"

Peele glared. "Can't you drop the subject, Salty? I explained the whole thing to you."

"That's what you think, or it's what you wanted us to think. I let it pass at the time, but you weren't fooling me. I was perfectly aware of the fact that you weren't telling us anything. You were lying, Louis. And you're still lying."

Peele sat erect, so utterly astonished at Salt River's unexpected revolt that he forgot for a moment just how furious he should be. "*What* did you say?"

"Oh, you heard me," Salt River answered, his voice level and unperturbed. "There are two ways of lying, Louis. One is telling what isn't so. The other is leaving out something that *is* so. That's the way you're lying. You aren't telling all you know, and you can't make us believe that you are."

"I never tell all I know, you poor fool."

"You can't be so wise as you think you are, or you wouldn't expect us to swallow the excuses you gave for your actions. If you were so sure that Gage knew where the money is, why didn't you take him into camp when you first came to Great Lost Valley, and squeeze it out of him? That's about your speed, Louis. I don't believe you really think that Hardin knows where the money is."

Into Peele's glowering face there came an evil grin. "Well, if you figured that much out, you might have figured further that I counted on the fact that some day he might know."

"Oh, yes, I got that far." Salt River was quite conscious of the silence that had fallen over the rest of the men, of the threat in the air, but he ignored it. "I even got it figured out what must be the one way he *could* ever learn of it. It was really Creegan who hid the money, and you know it. Nobody but Creegan could have taken it, you've admitted that before.

"But you know well enough that he never had any chance to pass the money on to Gage. And it seems to me I remember your saying one day that you let Creegan go to the pen when you could have saved him, because he wouldn't tell you anything about the money. You figure he might have gotten out of that swamp alive, don't you, Louis? Men have gotten out of worse places than that.

"And you figured, too, that for some reason known only to yourself, if he did get out alive he would look Hardin up. You weren't squatting there in Great Lost Valley just waiting a chance to search the Circle Crossbar. You were waiting for Creegan to show up. And you broke loose and forced the issue finally, because something scared the daylights out of you, and you didn't care what it cost you to get Hardin out of the way. What was it, Louis? Did you find out that Creegan was alive and on your trail?"

Peele's astonishment had turned gradually into seething fury. He rose to his feet, fists doubled, face paled.

"You've been thinking too much, Salty. You've——"

Salt River Charley got to his feet, also, tensed in every muscle, so alert that his features were utterly still.

"And just why would Creegan look up Gage Hardin, Louis? You said yourself that he had only seen Hardin once or twice, and that was before the holdup. You don't want Hardin in jail just so you can get him out and make him talk. Even a school kid wouldn't swallow a story like that. You want him in jail so Creegan can't get to him. And you know, and I know, that you won't tell the real facts in this Creegan-Hardin affair, the one secret thing that would clear up the whole puzzle. So—I quit. The trail is growing short." Salt River's gaze flicked to Dutch Sundquist. "I guess now is as good a time as any."

"And what the hell do you mean by that?" Peele demanded, startled at Salt River's sudden change of tone.

Salt River ignored him. It was Dutch Sundquist who spoke, softly, but very audibly, answering Salt River's implied question.

"One each, Salty." His eyes looked beyond Peele, to another man and another country.

"Right," said Salt River Charley.

By that time, Peele knew. His hand darted toward the gun at his thigh. There was a smile on Salt River's face as he whipped a revolver from under his shirt. He fired three times before their fire downed him. His first two bullets pierced the head of Dick France and the heart of Barry Lucas. The third bullet went wild. The same smile was on Salt River's face as he fell.

Dutch Sundquist had no gun. He had only the knife Salt River had filched. He drove it into Soapy Hard's side just before three leaden slugs stretched him on the ground.

Weeny Hatteras groaned, staring about with appalled eyes. "Only us three——"

"Yeah!" gasped Cookie Boole. "Only us three left!"

"Shut up, both of you!" snapped Peele. "We've been easy marks. They had that planned all the time. The more fools us for not watching them a little closer after Tamm Oaks blew up. Dutch gave the whole thing away a minute ago, when he said to Salty, 'One each.' He meant to give it away. He was throwing it in my face! Sneering at me. Laughing at me! Oh, well! There's no use crying about it now. Help me drag these bodies over into the brush. We aren't going to waste any time burying them. If they're not all dead they soon will be. Then we'll move on to the next canyon and get a little sleep before we start traveling."

Peele's brain worked slowly sometimes. That night as he lay down to sleep in a canyon a little to the north where there were no dead men to keep him unpleasant company, it did not occur to him to wonder why neither Salt River

Charley nor Dutch Sundquist had made any attempt to claim him as one of the men they took with them into the unknown country. And even had he wondered about it, there would have been no one to tell him that Tamm Oaks, Salt River Charley, and Dutch Sundquist had made a pact among them to leave Louis Peele to meet justice at the hands of Gage Hardin.

Peele slept. He slept the dreamless sleep known only to men whose minds are untroubled because they are clean of all guilt or stain—and to men who are utterly without conscience.

Cookie Boole slept, but the dreamless character of his sleep was caused by sheer physical exhaustion.

Only Weeny Hatteras dreamed.

CHAPTER XXIII

A MESSAGE FOR PEELE

FOR the first two hours of his sleep, Weeny's dreams were lacking in all continuity and hectically scrambled. Then abruptly the senseless phantasmagoria merged into a clear and hideously real nightmare.

He dreamed that Peele, grown uncontrollably furious, because of some weird argument, picked him up with one arm, gripping his legs by that arm so tightly that he was powerless to struggle, wound the other arm in a crushing grip around his arms and chest, burying his face against Peele's chest so that he was powerless to cry out. The dream was so real that Weeny was in an agony of terror—when he realized suddenly that it was no longer a dream.

His eyes were wide open. He was gripped in the precise position he had dreamed, in the arms of a very big man. He could see the dark sky and the stars over the man's shoulder. He was being carried swiftly, yet silently, and he hadn't the least idea where he was being taken. He still thought his captor was Peele.

Five hundred yards from camp the man came to a halt in a small, clear space in a thicket. He spoke above Weeny's head, and the voice that addressed Weeny Hatteras was not the voice of Louis Peele.

"I brought you here to talk to you. If you keep quiet and act reasonably, nothing will happen to you. Make the least disturbance and I'll feel compelled to knock you so cold that you won't thaw for an hour."

Weeny felt himself being loosened from that numbing grip.

"I—I won't make any noise," he gasped.

"Very well, I'll let you down then, but I'm tying your feet so that you won't try to run away from me."

Weeny made no resistance as the man sat him down with his back against a small tree, and tied his ankles snugly with a rawhide thong which he took from his pocket. Weeny covertly scrutinized the face before him, and he gasped again:

"Louis!"

The man laughed. "Not Peele. Look again. They used to tell me that I looked enough like Peele to have been his brother. I thought Louis was a great guy then, and I was flattered, but what I would always have to answer was that Louis already had a brother. And while we're on the subject of Louis Peele, I might as well tell you that I brought you out here to give you a message to carry to Louis for me. He's planning on moving north at daybreak, isn't he?"

"Yeah, he is. How did you know?"

The other man favored him with a mirthless smile. "I know every move you gents have made since you left Great Lost Valley. I had no trouble in following Hardin, he was making no attempt to cover his tracks—as far as Loody's store. At Elks Crossing Peele turned back, while you fellows were asleep, to spy on Hardin. From that time on I have been following Peele."

Weeny, his terror subsided, grew a little bolder. "Well, if you wanted to talk to Louis, why haven't you talked to him long before instead of just following us all this time?"

"That's my business. This is the word I want you to take to Louis. Tell him *not* to go north. About a hundred miles south of here and about fifty miles to the east, there is a stretch of rock in the hills where nothing grows but sunflowers and sagebrush. It is called Devil's Flat. There is a spring at the south edge of the flat. Louis will know where it is. And tell him he is to turn east at daybreak and get to Devil's Flat fast as he can ride."

"Suppose he won't go?"

"He'll go. And further, you can tell Louis that I said this: prisons and swamps can be busted out of."

Weeny whitened and shrank back against the tree.

"Prison—swamp—and then you—you're Creegan!"

"Correct." The man who had made himself known to many people as "Chuck Weaver" sat erect, and there was an untroubled smile on his dark, bearded face. "You can tell Louis that the message comes from his old friend Halvord Creegan. I'll meet him there at Devil's Flat. Tell him I said that there was no other way for him to get any part of that money I took from Harry that night. And don't wake him up when you go back to camp, keep this to yourself till he is ready to break camp in the morning. Now I'll untie your feet and you can go."

He removed the thong from Weeny's ankles, and Weeny Hatteras rose to his feet.

The other man towered above him. "Just a minute, before you go, Hatteras. Who were those men among you called Red Corcoran, Dutch Sundquist, Tamm Oaks, and Salt River Charley?"

"They were four of Hardin's men," Weeny answered. "Hardin called them the Four from Hell's Hill."

The big man started, and echoed Weeny's last four words in a tone of incredulity.

"Yeah, that was what he called them," Weeny affirmed. "They came with the sheriff after us——"

"I know all the rest of it," the other interrupted. "I only wanted to make certain of something that I already felt was true."

Weeny looked up into the big man's face in the moonlight. "Say, Creegan, what's between you and Hardin? What have you got against him?"

A smile crossed the big man's face, a smile that a much more intelligent man than Weeny Hatteras would have failed to read. "I have a debt to pay to Gage Hardin, Hatteras. And I always liquidate my debts. Don't ask me any more questions. Go on back to camp, and at daylight tell Louis what I've said."

At the first sign of day, Weeny felt Peele's heavy hand shaking his shoulder. Peele's voice, harsh and impatient, smote his eardrums.

"Come out of it, Weeny. We ought to be on the way north right now."

"No, not north!" Weeny shook himself and sat upright, recollection flooding him. "You're not to go north. You're to go east and south, to Devil's Flat. Creegan said so."

Peeble blanched to the roots of his hair.

"*Creegan!*" He caught Weeny by both shoulders and shook him violently. "What are you talking about? Have you been dreaming?"

"Well, *that* was no dream."

Weeny waved one arm in high excitement, and recounted what had happened during the night, in such a jumbled torrent of words that Peele could hardly follow him. By the time he had finished, the color had come back to Peele's face, and an intent and cunning light had crept into Peele's eyes.

"I guess that puts a different face on it," he said slowly. "Maybe those years in the pen toughened him up a little. He was always a soft-hearted fool, howling about not wanting to make trouble and wanting to pay his debts. Not money debts, you poor fool. That man has a brain, even if it did seem to be hampered by a squeamish conscience. If people were decent to him, he always figured he owed them something. Does that tell you anything?"

"Yeah, I'm beginning to see. But what did Hardin ever do for him?"

"How do I know?" Peele countered. "I'm not going to lose any sleep right now over what may be in Creegan's head."

CHAPTER XXIV

GASTON TALKS

On this very same morning, at this very moment and hour, Mary Silver and Doe Gaston sat talking in the kitchen of the ranch house on the Circle Crossbar. Doe pushed back his breakfast plate, preparatory to rising from the table.

"Well, Mary, we've a long hard day ahead of us. I'd better be getting out. I don't feel much like work. I guess neither of us has had a decent night's sleep since Gage left. I don't suppose he's having a very easy time of it trailing Peele, because I have an idea that this is one time that Louis Peele isn't leaving any tracks for Gage to follow. After shooting up the sheriff, Louis doesn't want *anybody* to find him. You know, I still can't figure his squatting here and pestering Gage the way he has for four years, just because he thought Hardin might know something about that money."

Mary's gaze grew thoughtful on Doe's face. "But I thought you and Gage had just about reached a solution of that riddle, Doe."

"No, we didn't, Mary. And Gage knew it, and I knew it. There was some big reason for Peele's going no farther then he did for four years, and then suddenly blowing up and running wild."

"You know something, Doe?" Mary accused. "You've been on pins and needles for the last two weeks. I've known something was up. What is it?"

"It has to do with something Gage told me in private just before he left. Something he did not want me to repeat to Guy. You know those three men who went to prison for life, after the pack-train holdup? Well, the one named Creegan wrote to Gage after he had been in the penitentiary only a few months. He was, you'll remember, the one who helped to bury Gage's brother Bruce. Hardin was still around that territory, not so many miles from where it had all happened.

"The letter was forwarded to him. In the letter, Creegan said that he wanted Gage not to grieve over Bruce, that he had buried Bruce as gently and kindly as he could, and that it was better for Bruce to be lying hidden in an unknown grave than it was for him to be living and in the penitentiary for a crime he hadn't committed. He said that Bruce had spoken to him just before he died, had given him a message and asked that he deliver it to Gage. And what Bruce had said was in effect what Creegan had just said in the letter, that if he lived he would be sent to the penitentiary, sworn into it by the lies of Peele's gang, that he was better dead, and it would be easier for his mother to bear.

"Gage said that it seemed as if there was a lot of good in Creegan, that there was something in him worth saving. Creegan said that he had learned at bitter cost that it paid no man to go crooked, and he wanted Hardin to know that if he ever got out of there he was going to lead an upright life. The letter touched Gage; you know how soft-hearted he is.

"He answered Creegan. He told him that he was glad to hear about the way Creegan felt, very grateful for the message from his brother, and he hoped that by some process—a pardon, or leniency for good behavior, or some such thing—Creegan would live to see the day when he would be free from that place. If that day should come, he wanted to make a new way of life easier for Creegan; he knew it wouldn't be too easy ever for any man discharged from a prison friendless, penniless, and alone. Hardin had a good bit of money, his folks had been fairly well fixed, and he knew what money could do to make life easier for a man with an uphill battle to fight.

"So this is what he did. He told Creegan that he had sold his ranch and had left Tenville and the Hell's Hill country behind. He was going to leave them still farther behind, he didn't know how far he might go, far enough at least to get away from things he didn't want to remember. But before he left there, he was leaving in a bank, in a town near the place where he was living then, the sum of five thousand dollars. It seems like a lot of money, doesn't it?"

"Oh, I don't know, Doe." Mary's eyes looked beyond Doe to that long-gone day, to the grief-ridden and bereaved Hardin left alone. "Perhaps an older and more seasoned man would have thought a few hundred dollars enough. But Gage was little more than a boy, he must have felt a sense of gratitude to Creegan because of Bruce, and I suppose with the heroic impulses of youth he wanted to make Creegan a magnificent gift. Gage *would* do it that way."

"Yes," agreed Doe, "I guess that was about it. He left it, anyway. He told the cashier of the bank that the money was for Daniel Forbes, a name Gage made up, that another man some time would come to get it for Forbes. He left with the cashier identifying questions and answers that were to be asked and answered, and the money was to be given to the man who could make that identification. He gave Creegan, in the letter he wrote him, a copy of those questions and answers, and told him the money would be waiting there if he was ever discharged from the prison, whether it was one year or twenty.

"After that Gage used to watch the papers, always hoping he'd see notice of Creegan's getting out. And Creegan got out, like Hardin hoped he would."

"But Creegan was shot to death in that swamp, Doe."

"No, he wasn't, Mary. Hardin wouldn't take the money out of the bank, after the prison break. He said it could lie there forever for all of him; it was a matter of sentiment. But, Mary, when all this boiled up in the last few weeks, I got to thinking, and putting two and two together. Hardin had shown me that list of questions and answers, he showed me where he kept it, so I could destroy it if he never came back.

"So I—well, I guess I butted into something that was none of my business. Two weeks ago I wrote to that bank, gave the list of questions and answers, said I was the man who had left the money there and wanted to know if the money had ever been called for. I got the answer yesterday. It said that a man had called and got the money for Mr. Forbes three years ago."

"Creegan! He—he called for it!" Mary cried out.

"Couldn't have been anybody else," Doe replied. "And ever since I found out Creegan is alive, I've known who Chuck Weaver is. But why was he looking for Louis Peele, instead of Gage? And why did he act as he did when Guy told him that Gage owned this ranch? Guy told me that for a minute the fellow went white as a sheet. I've figured that far, but I'm stopped."

"But, Doe!" Mary's eyes widened, and a dozen expressions crossed her features in full flight, and a whirl of thought stormed her brain. "Then it was Creegan who repeatedly sent here after Guy, reporting the awful crimes Gage is supposed to have committed! Is that any way to repay a kindness? Oh, Doe, it gets worse and worse."

"Maybe," said Doe. "I'm not done figuring yet."

CHAPTER XXV

AND in the same moment and hour, on the same morning, Louis Peele was saying to Weeny Hatteras: "For four years we sat around there waiting in Great Lost Valley, waiting the day that Creegan would come to light."

Weeny promptly proved that he had some capacity for thinking, himself. He returned Peele's gaze shrewdly. "Bunk! Louis, do I really look that stupid? You sat around here in Great Lost Valley for four years just *thinking* that *maybe* Creegan *might* have got out of Lobo Swamp alive? More bunk! Some way, you *knew* Creegan was alive. Time's getting short, Louis. There's only three of us left. Don't you think you'd better come clean with Cookie and me?"

At any other time in his life Peele might have knocked him down for that speech. But there comes to every man, high or low, vicious or incorrupt, a time when he is so harried by the drive of his thoughts, so confused by unforseen circumstance, so unsure of his own reliability and capacity to judge the wisest step that advice from any individual is a godsend, and he must talk to some other man.

That time had come to Louis Peele. He answered Hatteras without hesitation or evasion.

"Yes, I knew he was alive. I knew it only a short time after I came into Great Lost Valley. That summer, Weeny, while I was still looking for a few men to add to my crew, a fellow came drifting into the Valley. He said he was looking for a job; he'd just happened to come to my place first, so he stopped and asked if I could put him on. I thought I'd try him out; he was pretty husky and he looked as if he could take care of himself. I watched him pretty close; he had a

148

way about him as if he might have done something once that he didn't want made too public. I thought more and more that he was just about the kind of man I wanted to take on permanently.

"But I couldn't find out anything about him. The only thing I had to go by was his speech. That told me what part of the country he had come from, and it was a long way from Great Lost Valley. I finally figured that about the only way I'd ever get anything out of him was to get him drunk. Fear will make many a man talk when he is drunk. It worked. And once I got him started talking, about all I had to do was listen.

"And I found out, Weeny, that what was bothering him was that in the country he'd come from, he had helped a convict to escape. This convict had run into a swamp to evade pursuing officers, had got out of the swamp and stumbled onto this fellow's camp. The fellow had felt sorry for him, he'd helped him burn his prison clothes, given him some of his own extra clothes and his pack horse, to help him get away.

"But afterwards, this fellow got to thinking and worrying. The more he thought the more he worried. His initials were cut into the sweatband of the hat he had given the convict. The name of the store where he had bought the hat was printed on a tag glued inside the crown. Just suppose the law caught that convict, wearing those clothes? They could trace that hat without half trying, and anybody around there where this fellow came from could supply a description of him. And what scared him was that that might happen, and he'd get into a nasty mess for helping an escaped convict to get away. This fellow had been in prison himself once, and he hadn't any hankering to go back.

"He decided that the best thing he could do was to leave the country, leave it quick, and a long way behind. Leaving it a long way behind, he came to this country. Looking for a place that wasn't too thickly populated, he drifted into Great Lost Valley. His description of the man he helped get away couldn't have meant anybody else but Creegan."

"Well, I can see all that plain enough," said Weeny slowly. "But I still don't see what was the idea in pestering Hardin all the time. Just what did he really have to do with it?"

"Plenty, Weeny—and I'm telling you the truth now. I knew that Creegan hid that money somewhere. I figured he'd have it in for me, because when I went to see him when he was in jail before the trial, I told him that I'd swear to his innocence in the holdup and get him clear, if he'd tell me where the money was. I said that if he didn't tell me I'd swear to enough to send him to the pen.

"He invited me to go to hell, see? He knew that nobody sent him to the pen but me. And I figured he'd want to get me for it. So I got a good guard around me, fellows tough enough that I thought they'd do what I told them to when the time came. It was Creegan I wanted to get and take him apart by inches, till I made him talk. I was certain he'd look Hardin up. I wanted to get Hardin out of the way. It wouldn't have been very good for me to let Creegan get to Hardin. But it wouldn't have been very good for me to do for Hardin in any way that they could pin on me, either.

"So I kept badgering him, knowing he hated me, trying to get him in such a place that I could do for him and it would never be laid at my door. But he wouldn't draw. Seems as if he'd made a promise once that he wouldn't go gunning for me till he could *prove* I was a killer. Then, a few weeks ago, I heard that Creegan was at last on his way to see Hardin. I knew I had to move, quick, and not be too particular about it either. Rood's deal with the horses got him out of the valley. And snatching Mary Silver was the bait I strung to get him after me. Once I got him out into the hills, I wouldn't have wasted any time about filling him full of lead, and lying low and waiting for Creegan.

"But Doe Gaston queered the whole works by sending for Guy Shawnessy. I had to hightail to keep ahead of the law— after Shawnessy saw me and knew I'd had Mary grabbed. And that's the truth, Weeny."

"Yeah, I guess it is. You sound like a man telling the truth now. There's one thing you haven't explained. How did you get word that Creegan was coming?"

Peele smiled. "Weeny, the mail boxes out on the road are over two miles from the buildings on the Circle Crossbar. They're right within sight of the house on my ranch. Hardin's mail box and mine are standing there at the road, side by side. For four years I've watched the mail man go by, three times a week. Every time he stopped, I went right out to get my mail. Gage never got much mail, only advertising letters, and seed catalogues, and that sort of stuff. They didn't interest me any.

"Once in a while letters would come for boys on his ranch. Once in a long while he'd get a personal letter from somebody, but the return address was enough to tell me none of those letters was from Creegan. Then Creegan's letter did come. It didn't have any return address on it. Hardin never saw that letter. I burned it after I read it. It merely said that the writer of the letter had succeeded at last in learning where Hardin was, that he thought he and Hardin might have a lot to talk over after all these years, that he had got the money all right, and that he would be in Great Lost Valley in a couple of weeks or so.

"He finished by saying that he had been to see Bruce's grave, and that he believed between him and Hardin the two of them could right a great wrong, and that he'd explain that when he got there. He signed the letter 'Daniel Forbes.' That didn't fool me any. I knew it couldn't be any one but Creegan. And I'd have worked it out, too, if it hadn't been for Doe Gaston."

"But you're still keeping something back," Weeny accused

bluntly. "You haven't said yet *why* Creegan would be certain to look up Hardin, and why it would be so bad for you if those two got together."

"That," said Peele, "is something you'll never know. We can't stand around here talking all day. I've changed my mind somewhat about Creegan. He's had plenty of chance to get to Hardin if he wanted to. On the face of it, it looks as if he was going to play ball with me, and that he doesn't hold it against me because I didn't save him from the pen. Anyhow we're three against one, and we can handle him if he gets ugly. Come on, Weeny. Wake Cookie. We're on the way to Devil's Flat."

CHAPTER XXVI

PAYING A DEBT

THE man called Chuck Weaver had wasted little time in the interim since he had left Weeny Hatteras under the pines. He had gone due south. He had reached his planned destination at daylight. That destination was a temporary camp, where there was awaiting him a small, lean man with a dour face, who came out of a brush lean-to to smile in relief at sight of Weaver.

"Back again, eh?"

"Yes. And my errand is done. I'm free to get this other business off my hands. Pretty soon my last old debt is going to be paid, Billy. Did you see Hardin?"

Pitchell nodded, and from somewhere within his ragged shirt he drew a folded piece of wrapping paper.

"He sent your note back to you. He didn't write anything on it."

The big man accepted the piece of paper from Billy's hands.

"All right, then I will. I'll jot another message on the back of this, and you can return it to him. Where is he?"

"Traveling north."

"Well, stop him!" The command was sharp. "What did he say to you?"

Pitchell dutifully repeated his conversation with Hardin.

"All right, Billy. Now you have some traveling to do. See Hardin first, then see the sheriff. You needn't come back to tell me what Hardin says this time. It will keep till we meet again."

Pitchell received the extended note, stood for a moment

twisting it in his fingers, then he raised a quick glance to the other's face.

"What sort of debt do you owe Hardin, Chuck? If you don't mind my asking."

The big man smiled. "No, I don't mind your asking. I savvy, Billy, that you're one of the few straight men I ever knew."

"Me?" protested Pitchell. "I never did nothing for nobody."

"No? Nor anything to them, either. Let that pass. You wanted to know what I owe Hardin. I'd quite as soon tell you. I once wrote a letter to Hardin, from a place that wasn't very pleasant, a place in which I didn't care to be, a place from which I was determined to go. The chance came, and I went, and I am here. Hardin had had a brother. The brother was killed. I helped to bury him. And I wrote to Hardin, sending him a message from his brother, and saying that I'd buried him as gently and as kindly as I could.

"Hardin answered my letter. He said he was grateful for what I had done for his brother. He knew I had no money. He wanted to help me get a start. He left five thousand dollars in the bank for me. I went there and got it, got it in one-thousand-dollar bills. That was a sentiment which you wouldn't understand. And that is my debt to Hardin, Billy."

"And you're paying it!" There was thinly veiled disapproval and bewilderment in Pitchell's eyes. "You're paying it—by helping the sheriff to capture him and take him to trial for murder!"

"Right," said the other. "I'm paying it. You wouldn't understand that either. You get along, now, and do what I told you to do. I had a hard time finding you, Billy, as I told you when I first looked you up. But I still intend to see that you and I make a go of life somewhere, as I also told you when I first looked you up. Only, there are these things to be done first. If the sheriff asks you any questions, tell him the truth. I'll take care of the rest."

Pitchell did not move. "You don't believe that Hardin killed Finley and Harrigan, do you?"

The big man frowned. "I *know* he didn't. He held up the first store, if you could call it a holdup, but he didn't hold up the other two. How I know is none of your business. I do know, and that's enough. And that's one thing you needn't tell the sheriff."

He stood leaning against a tree, watching the little man depart on the fleabitten roan, his face dark and inscrutable.

Hardin was sitting by a small campfire, making a meal from a rabbit he'd shot. He was eating the last of the rabbit when Billy Pitchell rode out of the trees, advanced to the fire, and tendered the folded scrap of wrapping paper.

"Look on the other side," instructed Pitchell. "He wrote something else there for you. You know where Devil's Flat is?"

Hardin nodded.

"All right. Read that, then."

Hardin wiped his hands on a bandanna handkerchief, shoved the handkerchief into his pocket, and took the note with no more than a sharp glance for Pitchell. The note was much shorter than the one which had been written on the opposite side of the paper. It said merely:

HARDIN: You will know Devil's Flat. If you don't, Pitchell can direct you. It is about fifty miles due east of here. Peele is on his way there with two men. Sundquist and Salt River Charley started a fight yesterday afternoon and were killed, but they took three more of Peele's gang with them.

WEAVER.

Hardin raised a calculating gaze to Pitchell. "I wonder if I can trust this Weaver? He's concerning himself a great deal with my affairs. He seems to expect me to take his word without question."

Pitchell smiled thinly. "You can. He wouldn't double-cross any man."

"Oh, no?" Hardin tossed the note into the campfire. "I believe you told me once that Peele is an old pal of his. And yet, he plainly reveals Peele's destination to me and tells me to go get him. I suppose you wouldn't call that a double-cross?"

"I wouldn't call it anything. The whole thing is a mess, as far as I can see. But I know when a fellow is square, and Chuck Weaver is square. He knows the answer to all this. I'd bank on that if I wuz you."

"Your Chuck Weaver seems to know a good many things, as well as the answer to all this, as you say it. I wonder if he knows how that ten-dollar bill got onto my blanket the other night, when I needed food and a new hat."

"Oh, that." Pitchell regarded him calmly. "He said if you asked me about that I was to tell you, 'What do *you* think?' That hasn't anything to do with this. Are you going to Devil's Flat?"

"No. I don't believe I will. I have no reason whatsoever for believing either of you. I will not ride either for Lava Rock Canyon or for Devil's Flat. Both places would get me nicely out of the way. And would give Peele and your man Weaver a beautiful chance to leave me a long way behind."

Dismay darkened Pitchell's face. He started to speak, half choked, disappointment and dejection settling over him like a suddenly descended cloud of fog. "All right. I guess there is nothing I can do about it. I don't care so much about you, but I hate to have failed him."

He turned the roan and started to ride away.

Hardin watched him go, frowning and biting his lip in thought. "Hm-m-m! I wonder if I'm wrong? That wasn't put on for my benefit. No man of his caliber could pretend to that extent. He was sunk, knocked galley west, because I wouldn't believe in his Chuck Weaver. I'd better not miss any bets." He raised his voice in a shout.

"Hey! Pitchell! I'll take that back. I may be making a bad mistake, but I think I'll trust you. I'll go up to Lava Rock Canyon and see if Louis Peele has been there. If I find five dead men lying around there, I'll ride for Devil's Flat."

CHAPTER XXVII

THE POSSE

GUY SHAWNESSY and his four men were advancing from Harrigan's store, as Hardin stood there watching Pitchell depart. Every man resident in the hills for a radius of fifty miles was beating the brush and searching for Hardin. There were two men in the hills answering the description of the dodgers.

The searchers had found neither man. But they had done a great deal of riding and aimless brushing about. At the head of the posse, Shawnessy was swearing furiously over the fact.

"If there was a square inch of sign to be followed, they've wrecked it," he said savagely to Shark Hoaley. "They have filled the woods so full of sign around here that there isn't a lead left to follow. I hope they'll do as I told them to do, go home and stay there."

"They probably will," Hoaley replied, "now that they've done all the damage they can."

"Oh, well, we know one thing anyway," sighed Jeff Baker, trying to inject a little cheer into the atmosphere. "He's headed north."

"Headed north!" Shawnessy laughed. "There are a hundred places to the north in which he could hide so thoroughly that nobody on earth could find him. That's what I was worrying about. I knew once he got far enough into these hills, he'd have as many places to hide as a jack rabbit, and with all the sign wrecked by thick-headed man hunters, we're in a jam. The only thing we can do is keep going till we get beyond the territory they've trampled up, circle, and see if we can't cut fresh sign. That ought to———"

He cut himself short, as a horse nickered dead ahead of him. The posse halted almost as one man. The sheriff glanced at the others, with a slight, quizzical smile.

"Now what?"

"Another fool man-hunter, as like as not," Baker said angrily.

Shawnessy drew his gun, his eyes on the brush from which the nicker of the horse had come.

"Come out of there! Come with your hands up, or we'll rake the brush with every gun we have. Come out of it!"

There was a movement in the trees and the brush, and a fleabitten roan horse came into sight, a lean, dour-faced man on its back.

"You needn't go drawing on me!" the man protested indignantly. "I'm not one of the fellows who have been ruining your sign. I was coming to meet you."

"Oh, you were?" retorted Shawnessy, making no attempt to disguise his weariness and disgust. "And I suppose you know just where the killer can be caught. I've already met a round dozen of your breed, and followed a half dozen false trails. I'd quite as soon not hear any more."

The little man halted his fleabitten roan, and sat erect in offended dignity.

"I've no idea where your killer is. I ain't been trailing him. I have something to show you, and you'd better come and look at it. If I wuz a sheriff out looking for a killer, it's something *I'd* want to see."

Shawnessy scrutinized him with narrowed eyes. "Yes? Well, we may have different opinions about that. What is it you want to show me?"

"Dead men. Three of them. I don't know them. You might."

"Dead men!" echoed Shawnessy.

"Yes, dead men, sheriff. Three men shot dead and buried in a gulch. They haven't been dead for more than a week, or thereabouts. Are you coming?"

"All right." Shawnessy made a commanding gesture. "Lead the way. But don't try any tricks. It would be the greatest mistake you ever made. Do you live around here?"

"Yeah." Pitchell turned his horse preparatory to obeying the sheriff's command. "I live anywhere so long as it is in the hills. And my name is Billy Pitchell. I'm fifty-four years old. Free, white, and don't owe any man a cent. I've no living kin. Anything else you want to know?"

Shawnessy chuckled. "Not about you. That's a pretty clear pedigree. I'm guessing you know these hills pretty well."

"Like my own foot."

"And you know the people who come straggling through this territory, too, don't you?"

"I may not know them, but I usually see them."

Shawnessy remained silent for a moment, his eyes on Pitchell's lean straight back. Then he spoke again, in a voice that was the epitome of casualness. "Do you know any man in this territory who is named Chuck Weaver?"

"Oh, I wouldn't say I know him. We never know anybody, do we? I know who he is."

Shawnessy's gaze intensified. Had it been a concrete thing, it would have drilled a hole through Pitchell's backbone. "He isn't a friend of yours, by any chance?"

"No, not by chance. By intent. We both thought it wuz a good idea. You needn't be so curious about Chuck. He hasn't done anything."

"You're the second person who has told me that, Pitchell. I didn't say he'd done anything. I was just thinking that I'd like to have a talk with him. It occurred to me that if he should be a friend of yours you might tell me where I could find him."

"Sorry. I know where he wuz a few hours ago. But I've no more idea where he is now than you have." Pitchell lapsed into silence with that observation and nudged his horse into a faster pace.

Shawnessy accepted his silence. The sheriff hadn't served in his official capacity for all those years behind him without learning to be a fair judge of men. There would seem to be little doubt of Pitchell's matter-of-fact veracity. Shawnessy accepted it as such, for the time being at least. The men rode for a little over two hours before they came to the gully which was their objective. They were not aware of the fact that they were being followed, which was nothing derogatory to their sense of observation, but rather something to the credit of their pursuer's caution in following them.

Pitchell led the posse up the gully for a short distance, then turned aside and drew their attention to a heap of rock under the trees, rock that had been piled there swiftly and with purpose.

"The three men are under that rock," said Pitchell. "You want me to dig them out?"

"We'll do it together," Shawnessy dismounted without waste of time. "Come on, men. We have to see who's here."

From under the heap of rock there was disclosed by laboring hands three bodies buried in a shallow hole. The top man lay on his face. The other two lay so that their features were visible.

"Fitz Tracy and Finny Hogan!" ejaculated Baker. "Two of the worst in Peele's outfit. Shall I turn the other one over, sheriff?"

Shawnessy nodded, and bent to assist Baker in the act. As the body turned under their hands, they saw the dead face. Shawnessy started, backing up with a cry.

"Tamm! Tamm Oaks! How does Tamm come to be here?"

Baker paled to his hair line. "Heaven knows."

Shawnessy averted his face. "Cover them up again. We've seen enough. But I don't understand this. I don't see how any man of the Four could be alive after that night when Peele's men surrounded them. I saw Red go down. Do you guess it's possible that either Dutch or Salty could be alive yet, Jeff?"

Before Baker could make any answer, Pitchell sidled close to the sheriff.

"No, they ain't alive. You can see I told you the truth about these three, can't you?"

Shawnessy looked down into the little man's face. "Yes, that's certain. Why?"

"That's why I brought you here," Pitchell answered. "It's important. There are five more dead men in Lava Rock Canyon. I'm hoping you'll take my word for it. Those five are in Lava Rock Canyon just as surely as these three are here. I can take you to them if you insist on it. But you need to save time."

"What is this, Pitchell?" Shawnessy asked sharply. "A riddle?"

Pitchell shook his head. "Not so you could notice it. Two of those five in Lava Rock Canyon are Dutch Sundquist and Salt River Charley. I don't know who they were, but evidently you do. And Lava Rock Canyon is a good day's ride from here. Don't ask me to prove that. I tell you you need to save time."

"You needn't prove the distance to Lava Rock Canyon, at least," Shawnessy replied. "I know where it is. But if five dead men are there, and three of them Peele's men, there can't be many more left with Louis."

"Nobody's going to contradict that." Pitchell smiled. "He has only two left with him—Weeny Hatteras and Cookie Boole. I can tell you where to find them."

Shawnessy leaned abruptly toward Pitchell. "You know where Peele is? Out with it, then. Hardin is trailing Peele.

To find Peele is to find Hardin. If we can corner Peele and cache ourselves, Hardin will run right into us."

"I wouldn't know about that. Are you familiar with Devil's Flat?"

"No. I am not." The sheriff turned to his posse. "Does any of you men know where Devil's Flat is?"

"Yah!" Swede Thoburn nodded his head with emphatic vigor. "Ay could go to Devil's Flat vit my eyes shut."

"Well, it's there that you'll find Louis Peele," said Pitchell. "He started for Devil's Flat this morning, but he started from Lava Rock Canyon. You can take a short cut cross-country, and you will get there about the same time he does."

"Suppose you go along with us and show us the short cut," suggested Shawnessy.

"I can't. I've got other business. That fellow can show you. I guess I've said all I have to say to you, so I won't hang around. I'll be getting back. So long."

"So long, Pitchell." The sheriff gazed after him with curious eyes, then turned to issue brisk commands to his men. "All right, Swede. You know where Devil's Flat is. You lead the way. Come on, boys. We want to get there before Peele does, if we can."

The posse set off at a smart pace back down the gully, but none of them had the least suspicion of the lone man who stood hidden in the trees watching their every move.

CHAPTER XXVIII

THE LAST CHIP

HIDDEN in the shrouding verdure, on the ridge to the left of the gully Gage Hardin stood looking down. His gaze withdrew from the departing posse that had been led there by Pitchell to fix again on the grim heap of rocks in the gully bed. Pain drew his features as he remembered what he had seen there but minutes before. Tamm—Tamm Oaks, faithful to the last!

Hardin had deliberately followed Pitchell, with the intention of trying to get a glimpse of the mysterious Chuck Weaver who was so greatly interesting himself in the affairs of Gage Hardin. He had seen Pitchell join the posse. Unobserved, making his way through the shelter of trees, he had followed them all up the gully.

He had seen the bodies uncovered, realized then that Pitchell had been speaking the truth. Only an occasional word from the men below had been audible to his ears from where the thick scrub sheltered him, but he had very clearly heard Sheriff Shawnessy's startled cry when the dead face of Tamm Oaks had been revealed to the law officer's gaze.

For a moment, it had been all that Hardin could do to keep from joining that cry, so startled had he, too, been. But he had remained as motionless as one of the tree trunks beside him until the posse was well down the valley. He knew each man of them, but it was of Pitchell that he was thinking, as his eyes singled out the man riding with the sheriff, and dwelt on him.

"So he was telling the truth, after all," he muttered. "Apparently I nearly made a slip. Whoever this Chuck Weaver is, he seems to be playing a straight game, though for what reason I can't for the life of me figure. What *is* his game?"

As the posse moved around a curve in the trail and dwindled out of sight, his gaze left them and came back to the rock cairn below. His thoughts were all for Tamm Oaks, lying there so quietly, and for Dutch Sundquist and Salt River Charley, whom Pitchell had declared to be lying in Lava Rock Canyon. And Red Corcoran—gone, too, like the rest. The Four from Hell's Hill! All gone now.

And he knew that in truth those four, so loyal to him, for so long, had given up their lives in his service.

At last he moved. Working his way out of the thicket in which he stood, he returned to where he had left his horse hidden and ground-hitched, and rode away from the ridge, taking a roundabout course. But because he knew his way, long before Pitchell and the posse had emerged from the winding trail in the rocky gully, Gage Hardin had left it behind, riding at an easy gallop toward Devil's Flat.

As he rode he was thinking hard. He knew Devil's Flat. Nearly everybody who lived in that territory did. If Shawnessy had lived in that part of the country, instead of being there only rarely when duty called him, he would have known it, too. Hardin was banking on that, and on his own knowledge of short cuts to get to the Flat before the posse arrived, or as soon as they did, at any rate.

Hardin considered the most efficient short cut to that desolate flat, but gave up the idea of attempting it now. For to take it he would have to pass through an area that for several days now had been alive in spots with little groups of men searching for him, some called by the hope of the reward offered, but still others from a sense of duty.

The way that led across the mesa tops and through the timbered land, he considered as he rode, would be his best course. So, turning his horse at the far end of the gully, he took a direction that led toward the foothills of the towering mountains. For a long time he climbed steadily up the little-used, twisting trail, his eyes set ahead, his thoughts tortured.

An outcast! And he had done nothing! This last queer twist of fate seemed the hardest of all to bear.

Deep as he was in his bitter thoughts, though, not for one moment did he relax his vigilance. He must not be caught now! The end of his nine years of waiting for vengeance was in sight, and no one must stop him. His steely, angry eyes persistently roamed over the tumbled hills that loomed to right and left, his gaze flicking from them to the timbered heights and rocky piles that could hide ambushers.

It was a land that Gage Hardin had loved, but he had no time now to think of its beauties. The pine-laden air was heady and moist. From clumps of shrubs quail called and were answered as they scurried to cover at his approach. The blur of their legs as flocks fled from feed to cover went unheeded by his unseeing eyes. Occasionally a jack rabbit hopped across his pathway and leaped to cover at the sound of horse's hoofs. But he saw none of it, heard nothing except the voices in his own brain that told him of the wreck of his life and hopes.

Even the misty peaks that once had drawn his admiration now meant to him no more than that beyond them, across from the valley that lay between them, lushly green and peaceful, lay the Devil's Flat where a man would be waiting for death—or where Gage Hardin himself would meet it. All nature was at peace and calm—but in men's hearts were war and envy and revenge. Men were riding that day with death in their hearts.

It took Hardin longer than he had supposed to traverse the detour he had chosen, but he knew it to be safest, and believed he would be ahead of the posse, at that. Had he had the option of riding where and when he chose, he could have safely traversed the more dangerous territory under the cover of night, but this was a time when he dare not wait for night. Louis Peele would be at Devil's Flat, and Gage Hardin must keep a rendezvous there, too.

Hardin had finally been convinced of Billy Pitchell's veracity, though he knew no more about who Billy Pitchell was then he knew about the Chuck Weaver whom the inconsequential little man served. Anyway, it no longer mattered who Pitchell was, or Weaver himself. All that mattered was that they had been telling the truth.

He, Hardin, had one compelling aim—to reach Devil's Flat before Peele could get there. To do that, he must save every possible moment, watch out for every chance of ambush, and though he could take advantage of this little known short cut he would have to leave it and ride out into dangerous territory before he could reach his destination.

With what might have seemed vast irrelevancy, considering the present circumstances, he thought abruptly of what old Shark Hoaley had said—that a man who was afraid to throw in his last chip was a poor gambler. He smiled ruefully. Well, this seemed to be his last chip all right.

He reached out a hand, moving it in an absent-minded caress along the horse's neck. Another irrelevant thought. Could it be possible that this would be the last time he would smooth that silken neck of Chaser's? Anyway, he knew that Chaser would give of his best at the drop of the hat. He had taken such care of the horse since he had left the Circle Crossbar that Chaser had received little more than enough exercise to keep him fit.

Most of Hardin's time, since he had learned that he was a wanted man, had been spent in hiding, and in waiting for his chance to get Louis Peele—the one impelling urge in his life now. And he knew now, too, that when speed was required of Chaser that the horse would be fresh enough to deliver it.

Gage Hardin settled in the saddle, nudging the horse

with his knees as they moved down out of the heights. He leaned to Chaser's response of steady speed.

While Hardin was riding toward Devil's Flat, and the sheriff was on his way there with his posse, and Louis Peele with his two remaining men were all moving toward the same destination, Billy Pitchell unobstrusively detached himself from the posse and returned to the brush lean-to. The man who called himself Chuck Weaver was still there, pacing restlessly back and forth, absorbed in his thoughts.

He paused and looked up in surprise as Pitchell rode up and flung himself off his horse.

"I told you you needn't come back this time, Billy," he said quietly.

"I heard you," Pitchell hastily replied. "But there's something I have to tell you—something I thought maybe you'd like to know. The sheriff recognized the body of Oaks, and was willing to believe me then. He and his men started off for Devil's Flat right away. But I saw Gage Hardin first off, like you told me, and he wouldn't go."

"What?" Consternation darkened Weaver's face. "Why?"

"He was suspicious of me, I guess. The best I could do was to get him to promise to go up to Lava Rock Canyon. Fact, he volunteered to do that himself. He said if he found the dead men from his outfit there, he'd believe me and go on to Devil's Flat then."

Weaver shook his head. "That won't do," he said tightly. "You go after him again, Billy. Stop him and tell him I said for him to go to Devil's Flat. And don't ask me why, but be very sure this time that you tell him that the message comes from Daniel Forbes. Have you got that, Billy?"

"Yes, sure." The little man nodded. "Daniel Forbes. I'll tell him. I can catch him easy, I guess. . . . Are you going to stay here and wait for me?"

"I'm afraid not, Billy." Chuck Weaver smiled, indulgence

and appreciation in his eyes. Not many men in the world could command such unquestioning loyalty as this. And he added abruptly: "I've got to get to Devil's Flat myself. Got business of my own there."

Chuck Weaver started toward his horse to mount and ride off on the most serious errand of his life. And as he went, he muttered to himself:

"I am a fool. Why did I ever hope to achieve justice out of such a tangle as this? Because I'm soft-hearted and sentimental, that's why! Who but a sentimental fool would carry five-one-thousand dollar bills around in his pocket for nearly three years and refuse to spend them because they were a reminder of a debt he had to pay, and then divide them between two women who'd had their husbands murdered?"

He shrugged the thought from him. He was not regretting the loss of that money.

"Oh, well," he said, with a sigh of resignation, "what does it matter? The showdown is right around the corner now. Fool or not, I've started this thing and I'll see it through. . . . Come here, Coal!" He whistled softly, and the feeding horse raised its head and answered with a soft whinny. "Come here," Chuck Weaver repeated. "We have to travel, boy."

CHAPTER XXIX

AT DEVIL'S FLAT

GAGE HARDIN had gone as far as he could on the detour he had chosen and the last stretch must be ridden in that risky territory, as he had known it would have to be. Now he was riding directly into the country where the men who had known and liked the murdered storekeeper, Shamus Harrigan, had turned out to look for Gage Hardin whom they were assured had been the killer.

Hardin, however, had no way of knowing that the sheriff had impatiently ordered them all to return to their homes and stay there, declaring they were interfering with his own search for Hardin and that he would find Harrigan's killer if it was the last act of his life. Therefore Hardin rode tensely alert, half expecting that at any minute he would be confronted by man hunters who would not let him pass. And that, he was determined, was the last thing that should happen that day.

He had negotiated all the difficult terrain, and the going now was easy and he paid it no attention. But as he skirted the edge of a rolling flat, holding Chaser to an easy lope, Chaser's right forefoot drove into a badger hole. The horse struggled valiantly—but to no avail. He had cleared cleanly the mouth of the hole and the mound beside it—but only then to plunge his hoof through the thin crust of earth a few feet beyond.

Weight of horse and rider combined thrust the slender foreleg so deep into the treacherous cavity that the speeding Chaser was unable to extricate the leg in time to save himself. The forward thrust of his pace broke the leg just below the knee and threw him headlong. The horse struck the ground with such terrific impact, his slim gray head doubled under him, that Hardin was hurled against an outcropping of rock with stunning force. He lay doubled up in pain for several minutes, the breath knocked completely out of his body, before he could begin to breathe freely again and get to his feet.

When he reached an upright posture, he remained as he had risen, staring, transfixed. Chaser had not only broken his foreleg, he had broken his neck. Chaser, the beautiful slim gray horse Hardin had raised from colthood, was dead. Hardin's face slowly went colorless under its tan. It seemed for a little that he could not move, that he could scarcely think. Chaser was dead.

He walked slowly over to the gray horse and again stood still, looking down at him. The silver-mounted saddle and the bridle to match glinted in the light, the saddle and bridle of gray leather made just for Chaser. He knelt and started to undo the latigo strap. His hand touched the silver-gray hide. He drew the hand back quickly, and almost leaped to his feet.

"No, darned if I will! When a man dies with his boots on, do they take them off? Old Chaser! I never want to see that saddle and bridle again."

His eyes stung, and there passed before his sight the fleeting vision of a long-legged colt with a slim, beautiful head, silver hide gleaming in the sun, trotting at his heels, coming at his call. His throat felt thick, and there was a sudden perspiration upon his face.

He turned away quickly, and struck off at a long-paced, savage walk toward the east. Grief and regret occupied his mind to the exclusion of everything else, so that he did not think just then how serious was his predicament, set afoot, with every man's hand against him, and with Devil's Flat nearly thirty miles away.

No sound broke the stillness of the forest around him as

he strode on, save the little sounds that belong to such secluded places. A pine squirrel chattered. A blue-winged jay scolded in raucous accents. A red-headed flicker hammered industriously on the bark of a tree.

And Hardin walked. He walked mostly on the thick carpet of pine needles that gave forth little sound under his feet. He walked, skirting infrequent scrub pine thickets that spread impassable obstacles in his general direction. He walked a few times down stretches of trail and one length of hard-baked road that went his way.

He walked till his high-heeled boots became a misery, then he sat down on the ground, searched for a piece of flat rock, and knocked off a slab of each heel. That made walking infinitely easier to endure, and he went on with renewed vigor. He walked till the sun went down over the hills and the cooler air of the night seeped through the thickets and crept between the boles of the pines.

He made no count of time, for he did not care to remind himself how hopeless and perilous his situation was. He did not care to remind himself that Devil's Flat was still many miles away and that the incomparable Chaser was dead. So he traveled like a machine and tried not to think at all.

The moon came up and the hours waned.

Now, when we think of a man walking, especially in comparison to other men riding swift horses, the pace seems appallingly slow and inadequate. But so many things are to be taken into consideration in any given situation, and any one of them may be important enough to change the entire complexion of the situation radically. A man, especially when he is tall and has long legs fashioned for long strides, can walk a mile in twenty minutes without putting any undue strain upon himself.

Three miles in one hour. It had been one o'clock in the afternoon when Chaser had fallen to his death thirty miles from Devil's Flat. Three goes into thirty ten times. Ten hours after one in the afternoon would be eleven o'clock at night.

Could Hardin have walked straight onward for ten hours he would have reached Devil's Flat at eleven o'clock that night. *Could* he have done it. But he had been slowed by necessitated detours around thickets and boulder clumps. He had stopped a few times to rest and to drink from infrequent creeks. He had been forced to go down into gullies, to ascend slopes. His dogged advance seemed to him utterly hopeless, but he continued to travel steadily onward.

Nearly thirteen hours after Chaser's fall, at two o'clock in the morning, with nothing to light his way save the countless stars which had the sky to themselves now that the moon had gone down, Gage Hardin came at last to a low, barren hill that looked down upon Devil's Flat.

Hours earlier in the night, Sheriff Shawnessy and his posse had arrived within a mile of Devil's Flat, and had halted there, to wait until daylight, lest they run into ambush. An hour after the sheriff's arrival, Chuck Weaver had reached the rim above Devil's Flat, had circled the end of the flat, and had halted at the top of the slope above the spring in the willows, settling himself there to await developments. Neither the sheriff and his men, impatiently waiting for daylight, nor Chuck Weaver, across the flat above the willows, could see the dark shadow that was Gage Hardin, poised on the brink of the barren hill gazing down into Devil's Flat.

Neither could they see the other slowly moving shadow advance behind Hardin, which was a small man who had dismounted from a fleabitten roan and followed Hardin for several rods afoot.

Hardin stood motionless, gazing with narrowed and calculating eyes across the flat, where, at the base of the willows beside the spring, the flames of a campfire glowed like a beacon. He could hear faintly the voices of men beside the fire, but no word or tone was clearly audible enough to give him any hint as to the identity of the men.

"That will be Peele and his remaining two, there," said a low voice at his shoulder, and Hardin turned quickly to face Billy Pitchell. "I've been following you for the last half mile," Pitchell explained quickly. "Had to be sure it was you before I showed myself. Started to overtake you and turn you back from Lava Rock Canyon—went quite a way, decided you couldn't have gone there, must have come here, and hit for here myself. Sheriff and his men are cached back there about a mile. I almost ran into them. Chuck's around here some place, too. I guess that tells you about where you stand."

Under the light of the stars Hardin's face was grim. "No, Pitchell. Not till I know who he is."

"I told you once, he's just Chuck Weaver, that's all I know. And one of the whitest fellows I've ever seen. It was him who told me to stop you from going to Lava Rock Canyon, wasting all that time. And he said—maybe this might tell you something, I don't know—but he said I was to tell you the message came from Daniel Forbes. If *that* means anything to you."

Hardin went utterly still. "Creegan!" he told himself.

"I suppose—you're going down there and take Louis Peele?"

"Yes. I'm going down there after him, Pitchell. When I have him, if he doesn't get me first, you can go back and bring the sheriff up."

"I'm going down with you, see?" Pitchell patted his thigh. "I've got a gun around here somewhere. Under my belt, I guess. I'm a pretty fair shot, too. You lead the way, Hardin. Looks like we were close to the end of the chase."

"Yes, it looks like it. Thanks to—Chuck Weaver. Let's go."

And the two men started down the slope together.

They went slowly, to insure their going noiselessly. They approached the campfire under cover of the night and the deep shadow below the rim encircling the flat. The voices of Peele and his men became continually more audible as Hardin and Pitchell drew closer. Their creeping pace brought them at last to the edge of the willows away from the fire, where they were as unseen as the willows themselves, but had an unobstructed view of the three men clearly revealed by the glow of the flames.

"Well, I wish he'd get here," Peele was saying.

He was standing with his back toward Hardin and Pitchell, facing the fire. Weeny Hatteras and Cookie Boole were sitting on the ground across the fire from Peele.

"He didn't say when he'd start, did he, Weeny?"

"No." Weeny Hatteras did not raise his brooding gaze from the fire. "He might come any time. And I still don't like your idea of having a fire going so he can walk right up on us, after what you told me."

Peele gave vent to a short laugh of scorn. "I suppose you'd rather lie down and go to sleep in the dark, so he could walk up on us and have us cold, with us all sound asleep and no light to show *us* how to move? You make me sick, Weeny. You reason like a calf."

"Stay where you are, Louis. Put up your hands, all three of you."

The command came from the dark behind Peele, and he whirled to face it. He did not put up his hands.

Hardin stepped into the light of the fire, both guns drawn.

Boole and Hatteras rose behind Peele, lifting their hands above their heads. Peele himself seemed suddenly transfixed by sheer incredulity. Out of the shadows of the night and the willows, a small man stepped to Hardin's side. He held level one drawn gun. Peele, his back to Hatteras and Boole, took their support for granted. He muttered for their ears alone:

"You two take the little fellow, Weeny. I'll get Hardin."

His draw was lightning swift, but both of Hardin's guns spoke before Peele's revolver was clear of its holster. Peele's gun dropped unfired, his right arm suddenly powerless to obey his will. A bullet had pierced the arm; another, his chest. Peele swayed dizzily, then slowly sank to the ground.

"Neat work," he said, looking up at Hardin.

Hatteras and Boole stood exactly as they had stood since they had risen behind Peele and lifted their hands into the air.

Pitchell took their weapons and tossed them to the ground at Hardin's feet.

"You can drop your arms," Hardin said to Hatteras and Boole. "But stay where you are. I'm keeping you covered."

Hatteras spoke. "We haven't done anything, Hardin. We've been Peele's men, yes. But we never did anything worse than to cut your fence and to kill a couple of your beeves. We never knew Louis was so out-and-out bad till this last trip. Cookie and I would get out of this if we could. And nobody would ever take us in again like Louis did. We didn't have anything to do with the horses, or Pope, or with carrying off Mary."

"Why did you three come here to Devil's Flat?" Hardin temporarily evaded the issue of Weeny's and Cookie's culpability. "I have to know what I'm doing, before I make any such move as that, Hatteras."

Hatteras spoke again.

"We came here to meet Vord Creegan, Gage. If you didn't know that he'd got out of the pen alive, I'm telling you now. He was going to meet us here to divide the cash taken from the pack train. He hasn't shown up yet. None of us will ever see him now. And you can take it or leave it, but I'm not going to lie when you've got me in such a position as this."

"All right," Hardin said quietly. "You and Boole can go,

Hatteras. The farther you go, and the faster, the better I'll like it. I hope I never see you again."

"You won't!" Weeny Hatteras promised, with an earnestness that was its own verification, as he and Boole promptly disappeared into the willows and the shadows.

"I'll look after Louis, Pitchell." Hardin slipped his guns into their holsters. "You go after Guy and the posse, will you?" He stooped to pick up the guns and cartridge belts belonging to Boole and Hatteras, which Pitchell had tossed to the ground at his feet, and the gun that had dropped from Peele's hand. "Bring pronto." Hardin stood erect again. "I'm tired."

"You can stay right where you are, Gage, and you, Pitchell." The voice of Guy Shawnessy came from the darkness beyond the radius of the campfire's glow. "We heard the sound of firing. What's it all about, Gage? Where are Hatteras and Boole?"

"I let them go." Hardin turned quietly to face the sheriff, his hands at his sides. "Not two minutes ago. They hadn't done anything criminal, and I'd give any not-too-guilty man a chance to start over if he asked for it and I had my way about it. Besides, my business is with Peele, not with the men he forced into things they didn't want to do. And there's Peele. I had to shoot him to save myself. And that's the only time I ever shot a man, Guy, believe it or not. No matter how much evidence may be piled up against me, I had nothing to do with the Finley and Harrigan murders."

Peele laughed weakly. "What's the use, Gage? We're both of us caught. I tried to get a rise out of you, by letting my men run off your horses and shoot Lon Pope. I'll admit that I was the main one in carrying off Mary Silver, to try to draw you on. But outside of not giving her much to eat, we didn't hurt her. Doe Gaston had to send the sheriff after us, and I went off my head and shot the sheriff up. I suppose I'm going to the pen, and I hope you're lucky enough to do the same. I don't suppose you'll believe me, but I really hope you won't hang for killing Harrigan and the Finleys. To see you in the pen would satisfy me. And, you know, it —it won't do you much good to deny the killing. Weeny Hatteras and Dick France both saw you coming out of Harrigan's store right after the shooting, saw Eileen Harrigan chase you out of the store. Dick's dead, but Weeny will verify that if the sheriff wants—to—catch—him."

"Save it, Peele," the sheriff commanded. "Save it for the trial. That testimony is all we could ask to substantiate the evidence. We'll catch Hatteras and——" He ceased speaking, realizing that he was addressing deaf ears. Peele had lost consciousness. Shawnessy turned to Hardin. "I'm sorry, Gage, but it's all up. Maybe you can get off with a life sentence. I hope you can. Swede, step up there and take Hardin's guns. Jeff, you better take a look at Peele and see what you can do for him."

Hardin stood immobile and patient, as Swede Thoburn awkwardly approached him and Jeff Baker passed around the campfire to bend over Louis Peele.

Then a shadow detached itself from the other shadows at the edge of the willows and advanced a step, to become the dimly outlined figure of a man. From the shadowy figure a voice addressed Shawnessy.

"Just a minute, sheriff!"

The entire group about the campfire became a tableau, poised, startled, all faces turned toward the man who had so abruptly revealed himself.

"Stop right there!" Shawnessy commanded, and his hand went swiftly to the butt of his gun. "Who are you and what do you want?"

"I am Chuck Weaver——"

"And Chuck Weaver is Halvord Creegan," interrupted Shawnessy. "So let's don't do any beating around the bush."

"Just as you say, sheriff. So I'm Halvord Creegan."

Shawnessy stared at the shadowy figure. "You have made yourself very active in this whole affair, Creegan. If you see fit to explain yourself now, I'm certainly ready to listen."

"Thanks. I guess that's all I could ask. I've made myself active, as you put it, because I didn't want to see Hardin suffer for something he hasn't done. You see, it's this way. I owe Hardin something. What it is doesn't concern you. That lies between him and me. I have something to settle with Louis Peele, but that doesn't concern you, either. I got trace of both of them, and went to Great Lost Valley to see both of them. You answered the door that day. You know that neither of them was there.

"I was watching from the trees when Gage walked into Loody's store and asked for food. I was near enough to hear everything that was said. I was near enough to see Louis Peele there spying upon Hardin. That's where Louis got his idea. I knew he was up to something right then. That's why I walked in and told Loody to send for you. My sole object was to protect Hardin, not to hurt him.

"From then on I followed Peele—and kept a weather eye on Gage Hardin. The night the Finleys were killed, I followed Peele to within a few yards of the Finley store. I repeat, I knew he was up to something, but I couldn't guess what. I stayed in the brush and watched. He went into the Finley store, said that he was Gage Hardin, used almost the exact words Hardin had used to Loody, and shot the Finleys and raced out of there before I could raise a hand to stop him. Swede Thoburn came running down the road.

"I took a minute to speak to him, and followed Peele. And I wondered as I rode why Peele really had looked so much like Hardin in the light of the store windows, why his beard had seemed so black. I overtook him and continued to follow him. A few miles from the Finley store he stopped at a creek and washed his face. When he turned away from the creek, I knew. His beard that had looked black, glinted

reddish in the light of a match he struck to kindle a ciga-
rette.

"I knew what he'd done. He'd used something that would
temporarily stain his reddish beard black, something that
would wash off easily. He made capital of that not unusual
complexion of his, his dark hair and eyes and reddish beard,
to pose as Hardin.

"The morning of the Harrigan murder, I followed him
again. I was certain then what he intended to do. I was determined to get there in time to stop him, to kill him if I had
to, to save somebody else. I was too late. I did what I
could for Mrs. Harrigan and her daughter. Then I streaked
out after Peele. I managed to cut his trail and overtake him.
After I'd followed him for about two miles, he stopped, got
off his horse, removed his saddle from the horse, and hid
a lot of bills in his saddle blanket.

"There can't be any doubt that they were the bills he took
from Harrigan's store. It was Louis Peele who did the killing, not Hardin. I once said that the only way they'd ever
take me back to the pen was feet first. But I'll go willingly,
to save Gage Hardin the injustice of paying for another
man's guilt, and to see Louis Peele get what's coming to
him."

Starkly, the tableau still held about the fire. Motionless
men gazed at the shadowy figure, striving to encompass all
that had been revealed by "Chuck Weaver." After a long-
drawn minute of silence, the sheriff spoke.

"That sounds like the truth, Creegan. If it *is*, it's easy
enough to prove, though you may not know it. Any man
might stow extra currency in his saddle blanket. But I can
identify one of the bills taken from Harrigan's store beyond
question. From Eileen's testimony, we know that the killer
rode a gray horse. Hoaley, you and Swede go back where
those horses are beyond the willows. If there's a gray one
there, bring it. Have you anything else to say, Creegan?"

The man who had called himself Chuck Weaver glanced idly at Swede Thoburn and Shark Hoaley, who had turned back instantly to where they had noted the horses which had been ridden by Peele and his men. None could see more than the dim outline of Weaver's dark figure. None could see that his gaze went to Hardin, and lingered there.

"I don't see what it would be. I thought if I got you on Hardin's trail you would come up here and take him in— before some misguided fool shot him down, believing him guilty of the things Peele did. Because, after seeing Peele spying on him that night at Loody's store, I knew Peele was going to do something. And I really believed that, after Peele killed the Finleys and Harrigan, you, knowing Hardin as you did, being his friend, never could believe that Gage Hardin would commit any crimes as bad as either of those. I thought you'd go looking for the man who did it. I didn't foresee—how could I?—the way in which the evidence would pile up against him. I guess I didn't give Louis Peele credit for being as clever as he proved. But he—— There's your gray horse, sheriff. Look in the saddle blanket on his back, and, if you really can identify any of those bills, you'll know I'm telling the truth."

Shawnessy did not move, as Shark Hoaley and Swede Thoburn advanced into the light of the fire, leading a gray horse.

"The other two horses were gone, sheriff," Hoaley announced. "Hatteras and Boole must have made their getaway all right. This must be Peele's horse."

Shawnessy gave the gray horse one swift scrutiny. "Well, it certainly isn't Chaser. By the way, Gage, where is Chaser? We didn't see anything of him as we came in."

From across the fire, the voice of Billy Pitchell broke in harshly. "Forget it. Chaser is thirty miles from here, dead, his leg in a badger hole. I passed him and I stopped to look. I knew that silver-mounted bridle and saddle, too."

"Chaser, *dead!*" The sheriff's gaze flashed to Hardin. "Then how did *you* get here?"

"He walked!" flared Pitchell.

Shawnessy bit his lips, and his eyes seemed very bright in the firelight, as they turned from Hardin's face to the gray horse Hoaley and Thoburn had brought forward.

"Take off his saddle," the sheriff instructed Hoaley gruffly. "Lay the blanket over here. See if there's any money in it."

The horse was unsaddled by hasty hands, the folded saddle blanket laid upon the ground in the brightest light cast by the fire, while every man watched as tensely as if the fate of the whole world hung in the balance. Shawnessy knelt beside the folded blanket and flipped it open, to disclose a spread of limp five-dollar and ten-dollar bills arranged neatly between the blanket's doubled thicknesses.

The sheriff's hand disturbed the precise arrangement of the currency, overturning, seeking, and his fingers closed upon one new crisp ten-dollar bill.

Along the edge of the bill was written, "Lige Neumann, Meyers." Shawnessy rose to his feet.

His curious gaze went to the dark figure of the escaped convict. "If I could thank you, Creegan, I would. I can't. If I could let you go, I would. But I can't. You and I must feel about the same concerning Gage Hardin, only you had the privilege of putting him clear, and I didn't. I have to take you both in—you and Louis Peele. It's been a long time since that pack-train affair. Isn't there anything you can say to clear yourself?"

"Thanks. But I have no way to clear myself. Besides, I'm a jail-breaker now, remember? I can't get around that."

Shawnessy, the currency in the saddle blanket, and the convict himself, had so absorbed the entire attention of all the group that none of them had noticed Gage Hardin. They had not noticed how he had stood, rigid and motionless, staring with startled eyes at that shadowy figure at the edge of the willows.

They could not hear old and familiar echoes that sounded in Hardin's ears. They could not know that the big stranger had forgotten for a moment in his passionate earnestness to continue his effort to disguise his voice. They stared with a concerted and wondering gaze, as Hardin suddenly broke into motion, rushed around the fire, confronted the man who had saved him, head thrust forward, staring into that man's face.

Hardin, the man of quiet ways, the man who was not given to vehemence of speech, cried out, a wild and incredulous cry that echoed over the barren flat:

"Bruce! *Bruce!*"

Again the tableau held there in the night. No man could believe what he heard. No man save Guy Shawnessy, who suddenly saw the complete answer to the entire puzzle. But he did not move. No man moved. Bruce Hardin himself answered that wild cry.

"Yes, Gage. I——Oh, I planned something else—and my plans were all shot to pieces."

"Bruce Hardin!" Shawnessy had found his voice. "You —I—— Just what is this? *Are* you Bruce Hardin?"

"I am." Bruce Hardin laid one arm across his brother's shoulder. "I know what you're thinking. I'd have given my life to avoid this. When I started for Great Lost Valley, I intended to see Gage. I knew it would be safe, if I just saw him for a while, talked to him, and went on. There would have been something to live for. But when all this came up, I didn't want him to see me. I wanted to face no officer of the law. It's all been taken out of my hands. In spite of all I could do, he knew my voice."

The silence fell again. Shawnessy broke it.

"What's the answer?" he asked quietly.

"A few words will explain that, sheriff. When that pack-train was held up years ago, I knew about it beforehand because I had heard Louis Peele and his brother Harry planning it. I went there to stop it. I was too late. The thing had been done. I thought at least I could stop the robbery. Harry Peele had the box with the bills in it. I jumped on him. Creegan was standing right there. Jean Bluex yelled a warning at Peele, just as Creegan knocked me down.

"Harry grappled with Creegan. Peele looked back. He thought it was Harry and I still fighting over the cash box. He shot Creegan and Harry down. He thought I was Creegan. I was standing right where Creegan had been. He told Porky and me to bury them—Harry and Creegan—only he said to bury Harry and Bruce. Porky didn't know who I was, he didn't know any of the gang. He was a new man Peele had rung in that night. I had the cash box. Porky and I buried Harry and Creegan. Porky and I separated, to make a get-away. Is that all clear?"

"Perfectly clear," Shawnessy answered.

"There isn't much more. It occurred to me that I was in a bad spot. I knew Louis Peele. I knew when he found out, if he did find it out, that it was Creegan and not I who had been killed and buried with Harry, he might do any-thing. I thought of my mother, of Gage. I didn't know what might happen to me. I thought it was better for them to believe that I was dead than to see me go to the penitentiary if Louis had any way of sending me there. I knew by then how spiteful Louis Peele was. There was no hope for me if he got a chance at me.

"I thought fast, Shawnessy. I figured a way to save Gage and my mother from shame over me, should I be caught in the trap I feared. Should I reach home safe, and so keep myself clear of being linked to the damn affair, what I planned to do would be of no effect, because it would never be known. I went back to the place where Creegan and Harry were buried under the rocks and leaves.

"I shot holes in my coat and put it on Creegan's body. I put my ring on his finger. Were I taken before I could get out of the woods and away from there, I had decided to assume the identity of Vord Creegan. That was what happened. I feared at first that I might be recognized and my own identity brought to light.

"But the fates were with me, or against me—as you choose to see it. The county seat was pretty well to the north of the county, the Hell's Hill country was barely inside the south line. The sheriff had never seen me, or Creegan. He and some deputies from the north caught me there in the woods, and it didn't take me long to see that they certainly wouldn't let me go, no matter what I said. I looked tough enough, dirty, tired, several days' beard on my face. I admitted quickly that I was Creegan. They took me to the county jail. My beard is naturally heavy, it grew fast. I was sure that would help to disguise me if anyone I knew got curious and came up there. The people in Hell's Hill territory had never seen me with a beard. None of them came near me. And—well—I got by with it.

"Then Louis came to see me. The instant he laid eyes on me he knew that it was Creegan he had shot. I begged him to keep his mouth shut, for Gage's and mother's sake, at least until I saw whether or not I could get out of the jam I was in. Well. He said if I'd tell him where the money was he'd get me clear. I wouldn't. He said he'd swear me into the penitentiary if I didn't tell, that Porky had seen Gage, had shown Gage the bodies, that Gage and mother already believed me dead."

Gage Hardin repressed a shiver of revulsion, remembering. "But if that ant heap hadn't been there, Bruce! I was too upset to look close. I saw the coat, your ring—I couldn't bear to look at what I thought had been your face——"

"I knew the ant heap was there," Bruce interrupted. "That's why I told Porky we'd bury the bodies there. The plan was already in my head then. The iron box with those thousand-dollar bills in it is still there, in that ant hill, under the two skeletons. I always held to the hope that I might get out of prison. I intended to see that the money was delivered to those who had a right to it. Oh, after I got out and found trace of you and Louis, Gage—I made a lot of big plans. They're done." Bruce drew himself erect, and faced the sheriff. "I'll go back to prison if you say so, Shawnessy, and feel that I didn't make such a mess of it after all. Gage is free—and Louis Peele will at last get what's coming to him."

The sheriff's face was lined with distress.

"Bruce, I'd almost give my neck to get you out of this, but I'm afraid my hands are tied. You were there at the scene of the holdup. You took the money and hid it. You assumed another man's name and were sent to prison. You were sent to prison not for being Halvord Creegan, but for participating in murder and robbery. Gage would have to admit that he was not with you that night, that he did not know where you were. What testimony went on record, from Peele, Bluex, and Sidney?"

"Louis swore then, as he would do now, that he had seen me that night with Sidney and Bluex, riding toward the scene of the holdup. That he had heard us planning it and had tried to argue us out of doing it. Sidney and Bluex swore, in pure spite because I refused to tell Louis where I had put the money, that I was quite as guilty as they of both the killing and the robbery. And, after all—I *had* hidden the money. We're equally helpless, Shawnessy. Can't we cut all this useless talk, and get out of here? I'm in just as tight a jam now as I was then, thanks to Louis Peele. Louis Peele is——"

"Louis Peele is dead." Jeff Baker rose to his feet, across the glow of the fire. "That rather makes a difference, doesn't it, Guy?"

Shawnessy's troubled face flooded with relief. "I should say that we've all been having a nightmare. What are we blathering about, anyway? Halvord Creegan went to death in Lobo Swamp. How does that concern Bruce Hardin, living peacefully with his brother in Great Lost Valley? I wish you gents would all get things moving. We've wasted enough time in this——"

"One minute, Shawnessy!" interrupted Bruce Hardin. "Let's get it all done here and now." He turned to Pitchell. "Billy, what was your father's name?"

"What?" Pitchell stared at him. "Why, I told you, when you first looked me up. Marcus Pitchell. Marcus Aurelius Pitchell. I haven't seen him for years. I've always been a stray dog."

Bruce turned his attention back to the sheriff, a smile wrinkling the skin at the corners of his eyes. "The two prospectors who were killed by Louis Peele and his gang, Shawnessy, were John Hand Ogilvy and Marcus Aurelius Pitchell. Ogilvy left no heirs."

"So, that's where Pitchell comes in!" Shawnessy made a comical and deprecating gesture. "No more of this, Bruce! I've had all I can take in one dose. Remember that I've been a sick man. Come on, you jaspers, shake a leg. We have to hit the road to Great Lost Valley!"

When they did ride into the Valley several days later, Shawnessy halted them in the road a short distance from the ranch house of the Circle Crossbar.

"We are all staying here for a bit. Gage, you go on in, alone."

Gage gave the sheriff one long look, then he was gone.

"What's it all about?" asked Bruce, watching his brother's figure disappear down the lane on the gray horse Peele had owned.

Shawnessy answered softly: "Her name is Mary Silver.

She once embroidered Gage's name in the band of his hat."

"Oh!" said Bruce.

*　*　*　*

Mary Silver sat in the kitchen by the table, her head in her hands. Doe Gaston sat across from her. Mary heard the sound first.

"A horse coming, Doe. Could it be—any word?"

"I'll look."

Doe had reached the window, and the horseman had reached the yard. Doe's eyes widened. His color faded. He choked over stumbling words.

"I—you—just wait a minute—wait."

Mary did not raise her head. She heard Doe step to the door. She did not hear the door open, or Doe's lighter footfalls as he passed from the room. She heard other steps leap up on the back porch. She started and lifted her face then. Doe had disappeared from sight. Gage Hardin was standing in the doorway. She cried out, and got to her feet, the tears raining down her face. As Hardin's arms went around her, Doe Gaston closed the door.

THE END

Eli(za) Colter was born in Portland, Oregon. At the age of thirteen she was afflicted for a time by blindness, an experience that taught her to "drill out" her own education for the remainder of her life. Although her first story was published under a *nom de plume* in 1918, she felt her career as a professional really began when she sold her first story to *Black Mask Magazine* in 1922. Her style clearly indicates a penchant for what is termed the "hard-boiled school" in stories that display a gritty, tough, violent world. Sometimes there are episodes that become littered with bodies. Over the course of a career that spanned nearly four decades, Colter wrote more than 300 stories and serials, mostly Western fiction. She appeared regularly in thirty-seven different magazines, including slick publications like *Liberty*, and was showcased on the covers of Fiction House's *Lariat Story Magazine* along with the like of Walt Coburn. She published seven hardcover Western novels. Colter was particularly adept at crafting complex and intricate plots set against traditional Western storylines of her day—range wars, cattlemen vs. homesteaders, and switched identities. Yet, no matter what the plot, she somehow always managed to include the unexpected and unconventional, as she did in her best novels, such as *Outcast of Lazy S* (1933) or *Cañon Rattlers* (1939).